Step-Ball-Change

Also by Jeanne Ray
in Large Print:

Julie and Romeo

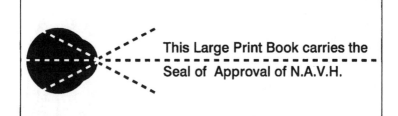

This Large Print Book carries the
Seal of Approval of N.A.V.H.

Step-Ball-Change

Jeanne Ray

Thorndike Press • Waterville, Maine

Published in 2002 by arrangement with Crown Publishers, a division of Random House, Inc.

Thorndike Press Large Print Core Series.

The tree indicium is a trademark of Thorndike Press.

The text of this Large Print edition is unabridged.
Other aspects of the book may vary from the original edition.

Jacket design by Franni Vitolo.

Set in 16 pt. Plantin by Minnie B. Raven.

Printed in the United States on permanent paper.

Library of Congress Cataloging-in-Publication Data

Ray, Jeanne.
    Step-ball-change / Jeanne Ray.
      p. cm.
    ISBN 0-7862-4371-6 (lg. print : hc : alk. paper)
  1. Married people — Fiction.   2. Triangles (Interpersonal relations) — Fiction.   3. Raleigh (N.C.) — Fiction.
  4. Atlanta (Ga.) — Fiction.   5. Rich people — Fiction.
  6. Divorce — Fiction.   7. Large type books.   I. Title.
PS3568.A915 S74 2002b
  813′.6—dc21   2002190359

For my mother Eva Wilkinson
Thanks, Mom

Happiness in marriage is entirely a matter of chance.
— Jane Austen, *Pride and Prejudice*

When your parachute strap is beginning to snap,
smile a big smile and tap, tap,
tap your troubles away.
— Jerry Herman, *Mack and Mabel*

chapter one

It all started on Tuesday night. Tom and I were having dinner when the phone rang.

Let me stop here for a minute. I want to revel in that sentence. *Tom and I were having dinner.* It almost sounds like this was something that happened regularly. In fact, my husband, who is a public defender, had made a career of eating peanut-butter-cheese crackers from the vending machine in the Raleigh courthouse while he went over the testimony of guys named Spit one more time. I had been teaching adult tap classes in the evenings to young women who didn't have a date after work and were trying to improve themselves. That was not to say I was never home or Tom was never home, but it was hard to make it home simultaneously, and it was nearly impossible to be home alone. Our two oldest sons, Henry and Charlie, were married and gone, but George, our youngest, was still down the hall while he went to law school. Kay, our daughter, found her way over most nights to review cases with her father. And if none of the children were here, you could count on the fact that Woodrow, our contractor, and a couple of the plaster guys who worked for him would be sitting on the back porch having some fast food in the evening. Originally, Woodrow had come to build a glassed-in porch on the house, what we called a Florida room, but halfway through the project he discovered that our foundation had shifted, and suddenly the cracks that were deep below the ground were spreading across our walls like ambitious ivy. The Florida room was abandoned in favor of the more pressing problems, and now stood as a naked frame of skinny poles on the side of our house. We had been under construction for six weeks, and I had come to think of the workmen as distant relatives who wanted to leave but had no place else to go.

But tonight the house was dark. When Tom and I called out no one answered back. Woodrow was gone and George was gone and the drop cloths were neatly folded and stacked. To further raise the odds on the rarity of this evening, I had actually bought the ingredients to make a pasta dish with olives and real tuna that I had seen in a magazine. So when I say, "Tom and I were having dinner," I mean it was hot food, and we were alone together. Tom had been so hopeful as to put on a Stan Getz record, and "Girl from Ipanema" laced the air. The whole evening was a kind of far-fetched coincidence. There was potential-for-romance written all over it.

But there was a second half to that sentence: *The phone rang.*

Tom answered it and for a while after hello, he said nothing. He just listened with a puzzled expression that could mean he'd been snagged either by someone who wanted to steam-clean our carpets or by a very distant cousin whose kid was in jail. Public defenders were modern-day priests in a sense: If someone had done something wrong, they were quick to call Tom and confess. Then he started to say, "Kay? Kay?" and then listened again. He said, "Honey, are you all right? Take a breath. Try to take a breath. Are you all right?"

Words to make any mother put down her fork and jump to her feet. I gestured for him to give me the phone.

"Kay?" Tom said. "Do you think you could talk to your mother? I'm going to put your mother on the phone." Tom's voice sounded frightened. He had a better sense of the terrible things that can happen in the world than most people do. "She's crying," he said, holding his hand over the mouthpiece. "I can't tell what she's saying."

"Kay?" I said. "Kay-bird?"

From the other end of the line there was a great deal of sobbing and snuffling, and immediately I felt my shoulders drop with relaxation. It was a sobbing and snuffling I knew. I can't explain how. It was as if I came equipped with the secret decoder ring that made me capable of distinguishing the intent of my daughter's cries. Even when she was a baby, I could tell from the other side of the house when she was hungry and when she needed changing and when she just wanted to be picked up and brought along for the ride. I could separate the cries of our three sons, too, but the difference was they stopped crying when they hit a certain age and Kay remained weepy by nature. Even now that she was thirty and a lawyer herself, she would find herself tearing up over an article in the newspaper or a commercial for long-distance service and have to excuse herself for a moment to go into another room and pull it together.

This crying, the subtle combination of gasping and a low, mucousy rattle that meant she wasn't even taking the time to blow her nose, I knew to be a cry over love. I mouthed the word to Tom, "Dumped." He raised his eyebrows and gave a sage shrug. Although it was a shame to think that such a thing had happened, neither of us was exactly surprised. Portraits of both Trey Bennett's great-grandfather and his great-great-grandfather hung in what they called the library of the country club. I had seen them over the years at wedding receptions and other inescapable social obligations. All the firstborn Bennett sons were named Conrad, though the grandfather was called Sergeant and the father was called, even on the most formal of occasions, Sport, and Trey was called Trey, indicating, one would think, that he was the third when in fact he must have been the sixth or seventh. The Bennett family was exhausting and inescapable in Raleigh, huge and recklessly blessed. They all had perfect teeth and Mercedes SUVs. They flew their own planes to their own summer houses and ski chalets. Their name was chipped into the marble of every hospital, art museum, and social register in the tri-city area. From what I could track in the paper over the years, they tended to marry young and reproduce enthusiastically, so Trey Bennett was a bit of an anomaly, being single at thirty-five. He was considered by everyone, especially his mother, to be the very definition of eligible. What he had been doing dating a thirty-year-old public defender who didn't even know any debutantes, much less been one herself, was a mystery to all of us, and now poor Kay was sobbing, her heart having been skidded across the pavement at top speed yet again.

"Baby," I said. "Deep breath. Come on now, try to relax."

Tom sat back down at the table and started to eat the dinner that was already halfway to cold.

"I-baaa," Kay said. "I-baaa."

"It's okay," I said. I pointed at my plate and Tom slid it over to me. The pasta was getting stiff, but I managed to force a few pieces into a twirl around my fork.

I settled in and listened to Kay cry. Sometimes that's all a mother can do. Truth be told, Trey had made me a little uncomfortable. Not that he wasn't nice. He was extraordinarily nice. His manners would have made Cary Grant feel inadequate. But whenever they stopped by our house, I was always aware that a family dog long since dead had peed on our only Oriental rug and left an irregular stain. When Trey was in the house, I wished I hadn't come straight from the dance studio in my leotard and warm-ups. I wished I'd showered. The few times he came to dinner, he complimented everything lavishly, but I was always plagued by images of matching serving utensils and Venetian water glasses. After the third time, Tom and I decided it would be less stressful to take them out.

"Do you want to come over?" I said to Kay. I looked at Tom, mouthed the word "Sorry."

He shook his head. "No, no," he mouthed back, and then he made a beckoning gesture with his hand for her to come on over. Tom was a good father.

On the other end of the line I could hear

Kay put down the phone and blow her nose, which was a sign that she was in the first stages of pulling it together. Then she picked up the receiver and inhaled hugely. I didn't make a sound for fear of distracting her. "Married," she said, and then began to cry again.

"Trey's getting married!" I said. Tom leaned over the table. "I can't believe that. Oh, sweetheart, that's awful. That's too much."

"Me-e-e-e-e," she wailed. "Marry me!"

I stopped and cocked my head toward my shoulder as if this might make me hear better. "He married you?" I asked quietly.

Cry, cry, cry. "Asked," she managed to gasp out. "Asked me."

I clamped my hand down over the mouthpiece. "Mother of God," I said to Tom. "He's asked her to marry him."

The blood slipped away from Tom's face. Who knew where it was going. We saw it all in an instant, the way they say you review your life as a milk truck swerves into your lane of traffic. But in this case what flashed before our eyes was the future: anniversary dances at the country club, invitations to sail in the Caribbean, severe pressure to attend fund-raising dinners for senators who opposed school lunches and gun control. The phone rang.

It was George's phone, what we still referred to as the children's line even though three of our children were grown and gone and George was twenty-five years old, in his first year of law school, and less of a child than Tom or I had ever been. Under normal circumstances we would have let the machine pick up, but these were not normal circumstances. Tom rose, pale as Banquo's ghost, and floated down the hall toward the ringing.

"Kay," I said sweetly, trying to make my voice that same voice that had soothed her as a baby. "Are you going to marry Trey?" For some reason all I could think about were their names, Kay and Trey, Trey and Kay. Marriage was hard enough without rhyming.

The crying stopped abruptly and I could hear the scratchy brush of Kay wiping the phone with a Kleenex. "Of course I'm going to marry Trey."

"Caroline," Tom called from down the hall.

"One second, baby. Yes?"

"Minnie, it's your sister on the other line."

The statement was redundant, since my sister was the only person who called me Minnie and the very word, like my sister herself, brought up a sharp, prickling sweat on the back of my neck. I didn't know why Taffy would be calling without a birthday or holiday to pin it on, and I didn't know why she was calling on George's phone. I didn't care. "Tell her I'll call her back."

There was a long pause, Tom was saying

something I couldn't hear, and then he called out to me again, "I can't get her to understand me. She's crying too hard."

That didn't make any sense at all. I hadn't seen Taffy cry since we were in high school and our mother machine washed her white angora sweater that was clearly labeled *Dry Clean Only.*

"Kay," I said, "there's something going on. Taffy's on the other line."

"Call her back," Kay said, the last vestiges of snuffle clearing from her voice. "I'm getting married."

"Your father says there's something wrong." Tom was back in the kitchen now, working a thumb over one shoulder, which meant that I had responsibilities on the phone that was behind him. "Here, tell Dad about what happened. I'll be right back." I handed Tom the phone and hustled down the hall to George's room.

Dear George. Everything was so neat, the picture frames were dusted, no shoes on the floor. Even the papers on the desk were perfectly stacked. He had felt guilty about moving back home to go to law school, but I knew for a fact that he raised our standards. I sat down on the edge of his twin bed. "Taffy?"

On the line there was crying, and suddenly I could see from the vantage point of close comparison that there was in fact a huge difference between the crying done by a broken heart and the crying done by a heart that cannot believe its own good fortune. "Taffy," I said, "what is it?"

"Holden is in Cannes," she said, gasping like a trout that had just been thrown from the lake. "I can't find her."

My niece, Taffy's daughter, was an agent for movie stars in Hollywood and no one could ever find her. The best anyone could hope for was to locate her secretary, and even that was something of a trick. "Why do you need Holden?"

There was more crying, crying so real and deep that I felt for the first time in so long I can't remember a stirring of genuine love for my sister. I wanted to be there with her and fold her in my arms. Kay cried at everything, but if Taffy was given to crying, I would be the last person to know it. I could only imagine how bad things must have been for her at that moment if I was the one she was turning to. "Is it Neddy? Is Neddy all right?"

She put the phone down. Far in the distance of Atlanta I heard my sister blowing her nose. "Neddy left me." She sniffed and cleared her throat. "There. What do you think of that?"

I didn't like Neddy, but that was hardly the point. I only saw him once a year. Taffy saw him every day. "What happened?"

She sighed, which I read as her being

bored by such an obvious question. "What always happens: He took up with some junior executive. It isn't even a secretary they leave you for these days. Neddy has to tell me she's a junior executive. She's thirty-four years old. Do you know what that means? Holden is thirty-six."

I closed my eyes tightly, remembering Holden's second birthday party. Holden in a white linen dress with yellow daisies embroidered across the front, blowing out two candles stuck on top of something that looked like Queen Elizabeth's wedding cake. Taffy was wearing sling-backs and diamond studs with her Lilly Pulitzer, making sure everybody had champagne. Neddy was talking too loudly about golf and forgot to take the pictures, which had been his assignment. On the day of Holden's second birthday, the junior executive, my sister's rival for her husband's affections, had yet to be born.

"Oh, Taffy."

"The stupid son of a bitch. I always thought I'd leave him some day. I never thought he would leave me." She stopped and gave herself over to crying again and my heart wrenched in my chest. "I need to get away. I tried to find Holden. I could go to Canyon Ranch for a while, but I just don't want —" Her sentence simply ended. Taffy always got what she wanted, but she didn't like to ask for it.

"You'll come here," I said. "You know that's what you have to do. Maybe you can talk it over with Tom. He could give you advice."

"I'm not trying to beat a drug rap," Taffy said. "I'm getting divorced. I called the best divorce lawyer in Atlanta. When Neddy was telling me about the junior executive, I told him I needed to use the bathroom and I went into the other room and called Buddy Lewis. Whoever calls him first is the one who gets him, that's the way it works. It's proof enough that Neddy doesn't have a brain in his head that he didn't call Buddy Lewis the second he knew he was going to divorce me. They call him the Piranha."

She was still crying a little and her voice was muddy with tears. At first I thought she said they called him the Pariah, which was not such a good nickname for a divorce lawyer. Divorce. Divorce, which comes from marriage. "Oh, God, Taffy, I forgot. I've got Kay on the other line and she's frantic."

"What's wrong with Kay?"

I knew that she'd find out soon enough, but I thought this would be a tasteless moment to tell her. "I don't know yet. I just gave Tom the phone."

"Well, tell her Aunt Taffy is . . ." She looked for a word and then started crying hard.

"Just come," I said, looking down the hall

18

as if Kay might be standing there. "Do you want me to drive down and get you?"

"No, no," she said. "I need to pack. I'll come in the morning. Neddy is staying at a hotel tonight. At least he says that's where he's staying."

"Call me before you leave."

"I can't go to my friends," she said. "At least not yet. I don't know what they would say."

"So you come here. That's why people have families."

"I owe you, Minnie," she said heavily. She was clearly sorry about this. She didn't want to owe me. We said our good-byes and then hung up.

I was born Carolina Margaret Woods, called Caroline, named by my father for the wondrous joy that was University of North Carolina basketball. I realized at a very early age that I was lucky he had not named me Tar Heel. My sister came two years after me (she would later revise this to four) and was named Henrietta by my father. He believed that large families were unseemly, the product of poverty, carelessness, or Catholicism. When he committed to having two children, it never occurred to him that one of those children might not be a boy, so he christened my sister with a version of his own name and then started calling her

Henry. My mother rectified this through the Southern tradition of nicknames and called her second daughter Taffy (Taffy: see childhood photos, Taffy's hair gleaming yellow-white with the individual strands resembling nothing so much as spun sugar). For a while everyone thought that Henrietta would grow up with a multiple personality disorder, what with a father calling her Henry, a mother calling her Taffy, and a sister who called her by her name. But it was no contest. My mother prevailed. She put a lace canopy over Taffy's little bed and bought her a flock of pink dresses and did everything in her power to make her feel as little like a Henry as possible. And it would have been fine if the story had ended there, with me being Caroline and my sister being Taffy, but once my sister mastered language, she seemed to feel self-conscious being the only member of the family to be living under an assumed name. As soon as she was old enough to screw up my life, she began calling me Minnie, not because there was any connection to my name or my appearance, but because she had a crush on a certain cartoon mouse.

"It's sweet," my mother said. "It's her pet name for you."

"I'm not her pet," I said.

"Minnie, Minnie, Minnie," my sister said.

"Make her stop," I said.

"I like it," my mother said, and scooped up

Taffy in her arms. "Minnie. Sister Minnie."

And so my mother began to call me Minnie to make Taffy feel better about her own treacly name. When Taffy started school she was quick to tell the other children that my real name was Minnie, and that Caroline was just something I had made up for myself. Boys especially liked to call me Minnie. They liked to shout it from cars as I was walking home from school.

But that was a long time ago. It was ridiculous for me to have such petty thoughts now. Neddy was leaving my sister, and on the phone in the other room, my daughter was explaining the details of her engagement.

When I came back to the kitchen, Tom brightened up. "Kay," he said, "your mother is back. Do you want to tell her this? She's off the phone."

Tom handed me the phone and I slumped down in my chair. My dinner had gone rubbery, I could tell just by looking at it. It had acquired a shine.

"What's wrong with Taffy?" Kay said.

There was no point in telling her the truth either, not at this exact moment. "Nothing. She's just coming to visit."

"Visit us? Why would Taffy visit us?"

It was good to hear her voice sound so clear. She could always cry on her mother's shoulder, but she was more likely to pull herself together for her father. They were both public defenders, after all, and when they were together they liked to act like a couple of tough guys, rhapsodizing over drug busts in which no one had been read their Miranda rights. "Let's not talk about Taffy. Tell me what happened."

"We're going to come over," Kay said. "I wanted to just come over and tell you but I couldn't wait. I haven't stopped crying since Trey asked me. I told him I needed to come home and get fixed up a little. We're going over to tell his parents and then we're coming by to see you and Dad."

"And you're happy," I said.

"Oh, Mom, the happiest." Her voice was dreamy and distracted, as if all the crying had made her drunk.

After I hung up the phone, Tom and I just sat there for a while, staring at our plates. "What happened to Taffy?" he said finally. "She wouldn't tell me."

"Neddy left her."

Tom slid his fingers up under his glasses and rubbed his eyes. "I suppose that handwriting was on the wall."

I figured I might as well get it all out in the open. I was always of the belief that it was kinder to rip off a Band-Aid all at once. "She's coming here."

"For how long?"

"I didn't think I could ask."

He nodded slowly. I called it his courtroom nod. It gave the illusion that he was really thinking things over, but I could tell at this point his mind was completely blank.

"Should I put dinner in the microwave? Do you want to try to eat something before the kids get here?"

"No," Tom said sadly. "I think we're finished with all that."

chapter two

"Why didn't you warn me about this?" Tom said, picking the vestiges of our abandoned dinner up off the table.

"I didn't know."

"You know everything about Kay."

"You're the one who works with her. Why didn't you know?"

"She talks to me about police procedure. She doesn't talk to me about dating."

Tom was right. This was my jurisdiction, and what I felt was a sense of personal failure. How was it possible that I hadn't seen this coming? Kay and I were close. We cooked, we shopped, we confided all. Sure, she had talked about Trey, she liked him fine, but if she loved him enough to marry him, I would have known it, wouldn't I? Of course, my own mother hadn't known that I was getting married, but my greatest reason for having children was that I wanted to be closer to them than I was to my mother.

If I asked Kay how it was possible that I hadn't suspected that Trey would propose, she would tell me the story of my own wedding. It was the stuff of legend in this family, the fairy tale the children requested at bedtime three to one over Billy Goat Gruff. I was twenty years old, a junior at the University of North Carolina at Chapel Hill, studying English literature and dance. Tom was twenty-three and in his second year of law school at Duke. We had dated for three months and then there was an argument. I can't remember what the argument was about.

"You've got to remember what the fight was about," Charlie would say, and settle into his flannel sheets.

"I don't remember," I would say.

"Probably something to do with her mother not wanting her to marry a Catholic," Tom would say.

"Get back to the story," Henry would say.

A couple of doors were slammed, Tom stormed out, that was that. On the following Friday night I had made a date with a boy named Skip who ran track. I was looking for my shoes under the bed when the house proctor came up and knocked on my door a full hour early. I was thinking it would be Skip, that he had gotten the time wrong, but when I got down to the lobby, it was Tom who was waiting for me.

"We should get married," he said.

Kay, decked out in footy pajamas, would squirm in my lap. She loved this part. It was her favorite line.

"I have a date in an hour!" all the children would scream in unison.

"I have a date in an hour," I said.

Tom sat down on one of the sofas that lined the guest area of the girls' dormitory and looked at his watch. "I guess I could wait."

I sat down beside him and together we puzzled out what was to be done about my dinner with Skip. That conversation was as close as I ever came to making wedding plans. Finally we called upstairs and asked my roommate if she would go on the date in my place, and since she had liked Skip herself, she was happy to help out.

"I feel sorry for Skip," Kay would say. "He wanted to marry you, too."

"Skip didn't want to marry me. He wanted to eat a pizza with me. Once you get older you'll see the difference."

I changed into my lightest-colored dress, something pale pink that I had bought on sale for twelve dollars the summer before, and we went to see the judge Tom clerked for. Because it was not yet six o'clock and the court registrar was still in the office, he was able to marry us that night.

"And that was the whole thing," Henry would say.

"That was it," Tom would say.

"And then you were married," Charlie

would say, and with the comfort of his own legitimate birth wrapped around him like a blanket, he would fall asleep.

I don't know what to say about this course of events other than we were, in our youth, capable of a kind of reckless certainty that probably wouldn't be possible now. When he said he thought we should get married, I wanted to snap my fingers and say, Yes! I was thinking the same thing. In truth, I hadn't been thinking about it at all, but when the suggestion was made, it seemed perfectly right and so off we went, holding hands, talking about the studying there was to be done over the weekend.

My mother could not stop crying.

My mother could not stop crying and yet, five years later when Taffy married Neddy in the Christ Episcopal Church with a dozen rose-pink bridesmaids and a twenty-piece orchestra and a sit-down dinner for 328 people, my mother took me back to the kitchen of the hotel, lit a cigarette, looked me dead in the eye, and said only, *Thank you.* I did not have to ask her what she was talking about.

After that we finished school from the enviable location of married student housing. Tom got a job pushing papers at a big firm downtown and I taught ballet and tap to six-year-olds in pink tights. I was the unimaginably ancient age of twenty-eight when Henry was born and had weathered seven years of family harassment for not reproducing more quickly. "It's all that dancing," my mother said. "That's what keeps you from getting pregnant. I never should have let you have those dancing lessons." My mother genuinely regretted not foreseeing my reproductive future.

But I kept dancing through my pregnancy, through all four of my pregnancies. The first three were each two years apart and I wore bulky sweaters over my leotards, but when George showed up five years later, I said the hell with it. I owned my own studio by then, McSwan's, named for my husband, Tom McSwain, who had shown his good faith in me by taking out a bank loan in his name after I was turned down. Not that Tom was exactly raking it in. He had left corporate law by then and was working in the public defender's office, hoping for a chance to defend the innocent poor. He actually said those exact words to me the day he found out that he got the job.

My point is that we stumbled into marriage, into parenthood, into life. Twenty no longer seems old enough to me to drive a car, and yet that's how old I was when I was married. As I waited for Kay to come over with Trey, I kept thinking, She's just a girl, she's too young for this. But when I was her age I had been married for ten years and had two children.

"Should I put a tie on?" Tom said.

I looked at my watch. "It's almost eight now and we don't know how long they'll be at his parents'. It seems awfully late to be wearing a tie around the house."

"There's something about that guy. He looks like he probably wears a tie to bed."

I walked around the living room, nervously straightening up. "I'm happy for her. It's a wonderful thing, right? Kay wants to get married."

"She wants to get married?"

"Well, she's talked about it. All her friends got married. After she and Everett broke up she said she thought she'd missed her chance."

"Everett was an idiot."

I beat my fist into a sofa pillow to plump it up and was ashamed to see the exhalation of dust that rose in the lamplight. "You'll get no argument from me there. Personally, I always thought she'd marry Jack in the end."

Tom stopped rearranging magazines and looked up at me in disbelief. "Jack from the District Attorney's office Jack?"

"You know they're friends."

"I know they went to law school together. The man is a D.A."

"Stop it, Tom. Jack is around here all the time. If Kay wants to move, Jack carries the boxes. If Kay needs an article for a case, Jack goes to the library for her."

"That means he's a sucker, not a boyfriend."

"Well, it doesn't matter. She's marrying Trey."

"So it's fine, if it's what she wants. Trey's a good guy."

"Right. Good."

"We married off Henry and Charlie. We know the drill. Now Kay's getting married."

But when he said it my knees felt weak. Kay was getting married. I rolled into the sofa. Tom rolled in beside me and I put my head on his shoulder. "It's different," I whispered.

Tom kissed the top of my head, the universal symbol of agreement. A daughter was different. Kay was different. The Bennetts, the Bennetts were very different. We didn't say anything else for fear of talking ourselves into something or out of something before we had all the facts. We simply sat and waited. When I was young and used to dance in shows, I would feel a great wave of catatonia sweep over me as I stood behind the heavy velvet curtain waiting for my cue. Other dancers were hopping up and down, flexing their feet, stretching out tendons, but nervousness coursed through my veins like Halcion. While I waited to show just how happy I was for Kay's engagement, a dark wave came over me and sucked me down to sleep.

I am a genius when it comes to sleep. I am the freestyle champion. This time I took Tom with me, and when we opened our eyes, Kay and Trey were there, looking at us like a piece of puzzling installation art titled *Your Parents Are Asleep on the Sofa.*

"We made plenty of noise coming in," Kay said.

"Not quite enough, it seems." Tom tried to gently dislodge my head from the curve of his neck.

"We shouldn't have come so late," Trey said. He was wearing a beautiful pale gray suit and his tie was perfectly knotted, the top button of his collar still snugly fastened beneath it. He leaned over to shake Tom's hand. "It took longer than we thought at my parents'."

"They wanted to call *every*body," Kay said.

"It's a lot of people," Trey said.

I shook my head, hoping to promote the flow of blood and oxygen to my brain. I remembered to fix my face in the position of joy. I stood up and hugged Trey. He was boyish and handsome, with dark hair and green eyes. For the first time I noticed that he and Kay looked something alike, that they had the same sort of coloring, a similar slim build. They would be the kind of couple where people would say to them, The two of you look like brother and sister, a circumstance reinforced by the rhyming names. The

31

bright light thrown off from Trey's teeth helped to pull me from my torpor. Next I reached for my daughter, my beautiful girl. I held my arms open to her in a gesture of love and unconditional acceptance, but to me she extended her hand. I squinted. There was nothing to say. I think the ring cost more than our house.

Tom, seeing me stumble, made a very minor attempt to pick up the slack.

"My," he said.

"Isn't it beautiful? Isn't it just the most beautiful ring?" As she said it, huge, puddling tears welled up in her eyes. If carat, cut, and clarity equaled love, then she was perhaps the most loved woman in all of Raleigh.

I hugged my girl, pressed my face into her hair. Kay was never good at ballet, but I was glad now that I had forced her through a few years of lessons. She would need them if only for balance. "Beautiful," I said.

Because my formal engagement lasted under forty-five minutes, I never had an engagement ring. We had to borrow money from Tom's parents to buy our wedding rings after the event had already taken place. It cost forty-seven dollars for the pair and we've gotten our money's worth out of them. Years ago there had been talk of our backtracking and buying me a diamond, but in the end I knew I wasn't the diamond type. I could only see car insurance and braces and college tuition sitting on my hand.

"Well," said Tom. "This is really something."

"Trey picked me up from work. He asked me in the parking garage. We weren't even in the car."

"I don't know what I was thinking," Trey said, his voice a lull of easy charm. "I had just picked the ring up and I had it in my pocket. I was going to ask Kay over the weekend. I had it all planned, first brunch, then the waiter would bring the box over on a plate for dessert."

"But then he couldn't wait."

"It just popped out of my mouth, Will you marry me?"

"Right there in the parking garage."

Not that it wasn't a good story, but we were clearly getting the second performance of the night. I imagine when they told it to his parents they must have played out every gasp and sigh. Now it seemed a little too polished, a little too quick, the *Reader's Digest* Condensed Marriage Proposal.

"She said yes right away," Trey said.

"As soon as I could stop crying," Kay said. Kay leaned into Trey's shoulder, wrapped the non-engagement-ring hand around his arm.

"Do you know when this is going to happen?" I asked, but I thought that sounded a little severe. I wasn't talking about a tornado, after all. "Have you thought about a date?"

Trey smiled at me with what almost looked like love. "We're going to try for six months. Mother will have to call the church and the club and see what the bookings are. She says we need at least a year to do it right, but we really want to try to do it in six months."

"The church and the club?" Tom asked.

"Mrs. Bennett thinks I should just take off from work now. She says even with her working on it full time, she's going to need both of us to plan the wedding."

"You're taking a leave of absence to plan your wedding?" Tom said.

"Oh, Daddy." Kay let go of Trey's arm and went to stand by her father. "I'm not going to leave work. I'm only telling you what Mrs. Bennett said. Besides, she was probably kidding."

"I don't think she was kidding," Trey said with a huge smile.

"Which church and club?" I asked.

"There's going to be so much time to go over all of that," Kay said brightly. "We shouldn't even think about the wedding tonight. Tonight is just about the engagement."

"My parents will be throwing us a party," Trey said.

I was trying to remember what he did, exactly. I knew that he worked in a bank, and that he was unnaturally high up in the bank for his age, but that it didn't exactly count since his family owned the bank. Still, he seemed perfectly bright, like someone who certainly could have made it on his own if the circumstances of his life had called for it. Or maybe it was just the way he looked at you when you spoke, as if you were exactly the person he was hoping to see and he just couldn't believe how fascinating you were. It must have been a trick they taught in boarding school.

"Well, we should go," Kay said.

"You've only been here a minute," Tom said, but it didn't sound like he was trying to talk them into staying.

"You were asleep when we got here. You must be tired. It is awfully late."

"And you've got a meeting with Markus Jones in the morning," Tom said, sounding more lawyerly than fatherly. "You've got to prep him for trial."

Kay sighed in a happy Doris Day manner and pressed her cheek into Trey's shoulder. "I may not even go to work tomorrow. I may just stay in bed and look at bridal magazines all day."

"I'm sure Mr. Jones will be glad to explain that to the judge."

"Oh, stop it, Dad. You know better than anyone that they only show up for prep one time in ten." She kissed us both. She seemed to sway to some private music playing in her head. When she turned away from me, I half expected Trey to spin her around and for the two of them to waltz out into the night, the engagement ring and Trey's white teeth lighting the path before them. "Good night," they sang. More kisses, tender waves. I wondered if this was what it felt like to find out your daughter had joined a cult. The cult of the brides. Tom and I stood at the door and stared even after they had driven away.

"Let me get this straight. They get to pick the church and the club?" Tom said.

"It's looking that way."

"But you told me — I remember this distinctly — you said the daughter's family got to choose. When Henry and Charlie got married and we had absolutely no say in anything, you said it would be different when Kay got married."

"Well, maybe it's like this: The bride gets to pick and Kay is probably going to pick everything they want her to pick."

"But that's not right," Tom said. "That's not Kay. Kay doesn't give in on anything."

"Did you look at that girl? They say your IQ goes down twenty points when you fall in love. I think they take off an extra fifty points when you land South Africa's largest diamond."

"And what's with that ring?"

"His mother probably has boxes of them lying around."

"Well, she can't wear it to the office. Not unless he's hiring a bodyguard to go with it."

Tom's mood was going south. I could see the muscles working in his jaw.

"What's wrong with us?" I said. "What parents wouldn't be thrilled to see their daughter marry Trey Bennett? She's going to be rich and hugely adored for the rest of her life. That is not such a bad thing."

"If Kay wanted to be rich, she could have made her own money, she could have signed on to any corporate law firm in the country and been the queen of all billable hours. But she didn't. She wanted to be a public defender because she knew that there were things that were more important than money." Tom was climbing up on the soapbox of social injustice.

"Things like pleasing your father." This was not the smartest thing I could have said. Now Tom's eyebrows were down, and once his eyebrows went down in combination with his jaw working, there was really no talking to him.

"She took that job because she wanted it. Nobody does work like that to make someone else happy."

"I know Kay loves her job and I know she's a good person."

Tom shook his head. "I'm just tired," he said.

We went off to bed in a state of sensory overload. All I had wanted was to go to sleep, but once we were lying together in the dark we found ourselves staring at the ceiling.

"When we had Henry," Tom whispered, "I remember looking at him in the hospital, this little baby parked in there with all the other little babies, and I thought, What have you gotten yourself into? I thought, For the next eighteen years this person is going to be your responsibility."

I laughed. "I thought the same thing. I thought, One day this baby is going to grow up and leave and I'm going to miss him so much."

"I just kept revising the figure — after college, after law school."

"After he gets married."

"But it never stops." Tom turned over on his side and I slid into the warm place he had made for me with the curve of his body. He put his arm over my shoulder and pulled me in. "As soon as we get the house fixed," he whispered.

"You'll retire."

"And you'll hire a couple of extra teachers."

"And we'll travel."

"Just the two of us." It was our bedtime story, and I closed my eyes and saw Tom and me standing on the edge of the Mediterranean, the waves crashing on the rocks in front of us, the hills of Tuscany rising behind us. There wasn't a phone anywhere for miles.

chapter three

Tom was gone by the time I woke up. After forty-two years of marriage we had figured out how to be quiet in the morning. I pulled on some sweatpants and a T-shirt and went to see if I could catch him before he left, but the only person home was Woodrow, our contractor, sitting at the kitchen table with a bagel and a cup of coffee, reading the newspaper. I was thrilled to see him. When Woodrow took on our Florida room, he had no idea what he was getting into. He had scheduled other jobs and so for days at a time he would be gone. I had come to believe the house was going to cave in under my feet whenever he was gone. My peculiar sense of logic had convinced me that as long as Woodrow and his crew were working, the foundation would not collapse.

Woodrow was about my age. We had both grown up in Raleigh. We had lived not more than ten miles away from each other for most of our lives, but we hadn't met until we had both passed sixty and he came to work on our house. That can happen sometimes, especially when one person is white and the other is black. The years go by and you just keep missing each other. Tom had defended Woodrow's nephew once, a good boy who did well in school but bore an unfortunate resemblance to another kid who knocked over Exxon stations for a living. After the case was over, Tom and Woodrow got to talking about the sunporch we had one day hoped to add on to the back of the house. Woodrow was feeling sufficiently grateful to Tom and said he thought he could do it for a very reasonable price. Except we only had slightly less than half a room. Every now and then he would have his men do a little work on it just so we could feel it might actually happen one day. The rest of the time was devoted to the foundation. That is, when they were there at all.

"Hey there," Woodrow said, looking up from the paper, my reading glasses sitting on the end of his nose. "I picked up bagels but Tom didn't want one."

"Is he gone?"

"Ten minutes ago."

I poured myself a cup of coffee and refilled Woodrow's cup. I sat down at the table and Woodrow folded up the front page and pushed it over to me, but I just shook my head and pushed it back.

"I don't care what's going on in the world."

"Tom told me Kay was marrying a Bennett."

"How did he seem to be taking it this morning?"

"I've seen him in better moods."

"It was a pretty big surprise."

"If one of my girls had ever come home with a millionaire, I think I would have found something nice to say about it." Woodrow ripped off a chunk of bagel and soaked the edge of it in coffee.

"Not if you didn't like the guy."

"Tom says you all like him well enough."

I shook my head. I was ashamed of myself. "You're right, we do. I keep forgetting that. Don't you want some cream cheese?"

"They didn't put any in the bag."

I got up and went to the refrigerator and found the cream cheese, and then I got myself a plate and a knife.

"Kay's a smart girl," Woodrow said, handing me the bag of bagels. "She's going to do what's right. You don't have to worry about her."

"Like you don't worry about your girls."

"When you've got four girls, you learn to spread your worrying out evenly among them. It's better that way, keeps you from getting too focused on any one thing. The biggest mistakes I've made as a parent came when I started putting all my worry on one of them. Get your mind off of Kay for a while. Try worrying about one of your other kids."

As if on cue, the only other child who was still around for me to worry about made his entrance. George came down the hall from his room looking sleepy, his pale hair kicking up in half a dozen directions. More so than with any of my other children, I had a hard time coming to terms with the fact that George had grown up. He was the baby of the family and I guess I thought that meant he would stay that way. It was a huge surprise when we found out George was coming, five years after Tom and I had closed up shop on having children. I still felt guilty to think how much I did not want another baby, but, of course, there was no way of knowing then that the baby would be George. He was the best of Tom and the best of me, which made him a much better person than either of us.

"Morning, Mother. Morning, Woodrow." He stopped, put his forehead against the refrigerator, and closed his eyes for a minute.

"Late night?" Woodrow said.

"A very late night," George said, his eyes still closed.

"Were you studying?" I asked him.

"Do I ever do anything else?" George yawned.

"You're like my daughter Erica. I had no idea a person could study that much."

"I hope she's not in law school. I can't take any more competition."

"Erica's in nursing school," Woodrow said.

"Maybe I'll chase an ambulance to her hospital someday."

"Woodrow brought bagels," I said.

George blinked. "That might help." He swung by the coffee maker and then padded to the table with his cup full.

"So you missed all the excitement," Woodrow said.

"Don't tell me." George rifled through the bag to find a salt bagel. "You found termites. No, better than termites. The house is built on ancient Indian burial grounds and has to be moved to Durham. Except it can't be moved because now the place is possessed."

"No, it's still just the foundation," Woodrow said.

"Kay is marrying Trey Bennett."

George sat the bagel on top of his coffee cup. He looked like I had just told him a very funny joke. "Bennett as in the Bennett library and the Bennett outpatient surgical wing and the Bennett watercooler in junior high?"

"That's the one."

"I'll be damned."

Woodrow pushed my glasses up the bridge of his nose and looked at the two of us sternly. "You people could stand to muster up a little enthusiasm here. For one thing,

43

you might need to have a rich son-in-law to help you pay for all the work I'm doing on your house."

"The Bennett Foundation foundation," George said. "They could sponsor a charity ball where everyone wore hard hats and black tie." He took a bite of bagel and chewed it thoughtfully. "Or a foundation fox hunt. I hear that old Sport Bennett loves a good fox hunt."

"Except you can never get the little hard hats to stay on the foxes," I said.

"Glue," George said. George was such a pragmatist.

Woodrow pushed up from the table. "Okay, that's enough. You people have problems. I'm going to get to work." No sooner had he said the words than we heard his crew pull up in the driveway.

"But there's another piece of news," I said, suddenly remembering it myself. "My sister is coming."

"I didn't know you had a sister," Woodrow said.

"A younger, prettier sister," I said.

"Aunt Taffy is coming?"

"There isn't any chance you'll be finished by this afternoon, is there? I'd love to get the place cleaned up." I said it as a joke and Woodrow stood by the door and laughed. I've always had a weakness for people who got my jokes.

"I didn't make your problems, that's what you've got to remember. I'm only here to fix them."

"Thanks for the breakfast," George said, and waved before Woodrow closed the door. "It's a shame Kay isn't marrying Woodrow so that we could keep him in the family."

"Woodrow is thirty years older than your sister, and besides, I don't think he's ever going to leave."

"So which piece of news is more alarming, that Kay is going to be Mrs. Bennett or that Aunt Taffy is coming to see us?"

"It's a toss-up."

George took a long sip of coffee and then stared into his cup for a while, trying to come up with a true likeness of himself. "I wonder if Kay plans to stop sleeping with Jack now that she's engaged or if she's going to wait until after she gets married to do that."

I thought I must have misunderstood him, though I couldn't identify which part of the sentence could be thought of as unclear.

"Oh, come on," George said. "Stop it with the shocked-mother face. You knew that."

"Jack the D.A.?"

"I think he has another last name, but yes, Jack the D.A."

"Kay's been seeing Jack?"

"Seeing all of Jack."

I looked around my kitchen. There were

cans of plaster stacked up in rows. There were buckets and drop cloths and rollers. Outside the window there were four men sitting on my patio furniture looking at old architectural plans of our house. It didn't look like anyplace I knew.

"I always thought she liked Jack."

"She likes him," George said.

"I have no idea what's going on anymore."

"I guess even Kay has a private life."

I shrugged. None of this made sense to me. "I should get ready for work."

"It isn't a big deal, whatever it is with Jack. Maybe I'm completely wrong about it."

"You're not wrong."

"Okay, I'm not wrong, but I certainly didn't mean to upset you."

"I'm not upset," I said, and gave his hand a squeeze. "But I should get to work, and then I have to come home and get things cleaned up, not that this place cleans up very well. I don't want Taffy sneezing the whole time she's here."

"You're going to have to tell me about that, too," George said.

"I think after tonight you'll know as much about it as I do."

I tried to sort it all out on the way to the dance studio. I wasn't upset about Jack, not in the sense that I was upset about Kay sleeping with Jack. Kay was thirty years old. I knew she wasn't a virgin. What I was upset about were all of the things I hadn't known: I hadn't known that she had any interest in marrying Trey Bennett; I hadn't known about Jack the D.A. Jack Carroll, that was his name. I felt like I must have been doing a pretty poor job as a mother if Kay didn't feel like she could talk to me about these things. Then again, maybe when your daughter was thirty, she didn't really need a mother to confide in anymore, and the thought of that depressed me, too.

When we had Henry and then Charlie, I felt like I was just trying to figure out how to keep them alive: food, shelter, avoiding major head injuries. But by the time Kay came along, I was much better at the job. I was more relaxed. I was the kind of mother I wanted to be, the one you could talk to. And now I was finding out that when it came to the really big stuff, she hadn't been talking at all.

When I walked into the dance studio, my mind still going in a dozen different directions, a five-year-old girl named Poppy attached herself to my leg.

"I lost a tooth," Poppy said.

I squatted down on the floor in front of her. Such a gorgeous child, black haired and freckled. "Where did you lose it?"

"Right in my hand," she said, and she opened the little drawstring bag she wore around her neck and produced the missing tooth, a tiny chunk of ivory.

"How could it be lost?" I said, touching the tip of my finger to the tiny incisor. "It's right here."

Poppy looked at the tooth and then looked at me, puzzled. "I lost it out of my head," she said finally.

And I thought, The world is still full of little girls who want to talk to me, so things can't be too bad. Some days they rushed out into the parking lot and clustered around my car while I unfastened my seat belt. Their sentences began long before I had the door open. "Mrs. McSwan," they would say, "look at my new tights, my new shoes. Look, Mrs. McSwan, I cut my hair. I can do the splits today." And down they would go, legs splayed across the dirty asphalt. I leaned over and hoisted Katie Chundra back up to her feet and she beamed at the touch. They wanted nothing more than my attention, the opportunity to confide in me, to stand beside me in front of the mirror. They raised their hands to speak even when class wasn't in session. They waved them back and forth like flags of unconditional surrender. Every minute I was there I heard my name spoken with burning urgency, "Mrs. McSwan! Mrs. McSwan!"

Or, I should say, I heard some version of my name. I had given up trying to explain that my name was actually McSwain a long time ago. They were too young for puns anyway, and the idea that they could be attending a school based on a spelling error would have been deeply upsetting to them.

I clapped my hands and they came running, the whole room filled with the slap of tiny feet wrapped in soft pink leather.

Tom was going to be sixty-five in March and he planned to eat a piece of birthday cake and hand in his resignation. He was going to walk away from the public defender's office the day his first pension check was ready, and while we traveled through Italy he would read all those big Russian novels that he had been lugging around since college. But me, I wanted to be buried at McSwan's. I wanted to be one of those ancient ballet instructors who shouted for *relevés* from her wheelchair, who tapped time out on the floor with her cane. I knew why the Rolling Stones kept going on tour long past the age when it was appropriate to be a rock star. It wasn't about the money. It was the love. Once you get used to the adoration and love of a room full of people, even if it's a small room with very small people, well, there is no giving it up.

This morning it was the bumblebee class, four- and five-year-olds, girls who had yet to be touched by the rigors of first grade. We made like daisies, stretched up slowly toward the sun and waggled our fingers at the over-head lights. I found something graceful and flowerlike in every child there, and if my daughter was marrying rich and my sister was coming to stay with me, for a while I forgot about it completely.

I was on to the second level of the exercise, where the daisies encounter a breeze, when I noticed that one of the flowers was larger than I was. It was George, his black warm-ups rolled at his waist, an old A.B.T. T-shirt with a faded-out picture of Suzanne Farrell on the front. He had managed to sneak in quietly, when all of our faces were thrown back to greet the sun, and when the girls saw him, they let out a high-pitched yell and stamped their feet. Only the very bravest of my students were able to go and throw their arms around George's legs the way they wanted to. They were all too in love with him.

"Reach, reach!" he said, his voice set to just the right pitch for the four- and five-year-old crowd, enough enthusiasm to make them work, not so much that they simply spin out of control. "Keep reaching!" He went up on his toes and came close to brushing his fingers against the fluorescent lights. My students squealed in appreciation of his height.

I gave birth to four children and ultimately Tom got every single one. "It wasn't a contest," he liked to say with the cool noblesse oblige of someone who's already won. Henry, our oldest and most practical, was a tax attorney. Charlie, the entrepreneur, was in real-estate law (which almost counted as a failure in Tom's eyes, though he managed to keep it to himself). Kay, the greatest source of pride, was making slave wages in the P.D.'s office just like her father. And it wasn't just that they were all lawyers. None of the first three of the children could dance. Despite the nine months of dancing they did in utero, despite the constant sound track of danceable beats that had permeated our home since their first hours of life, despite the fact that they came to every class I taught and were piled in the corner on a high bed of discarded coats and backpacks until they were old enough to take to the floor themselves, they could not dance. I mean, they really could not dance. The second I brought them home from class, they would shimmy up into their father's big chair, put their arms around his neck, and ask to hear again the story of *Brown* v. *Board of Education*.

Except George. The first time I saw him stand at the barre in fifth position, I thought that maybe the spell had been broken. Maybe I had pushed all of the little lawyers from my body. George was graceful and strong. He had a great understanding of music. Most of all, he possessed the single quality that allows boys to dance: He was completely impervious to teasing. When he was older and the boys on the football team said he was gay, George only smiled and winked at them. After all, he was dating every girl in town who possessed good posture and a pair of tights. By the time he was sixteen, he was teaching the introductory classes himself. He went to dance camps in the summer. He came to the studio at the crack of dawn to practice. Scouts from the big companies were coming to see him. George was going to be my legacy.

Four children. Four lawyers. He waited a long time to tell me, and when he finally did, what could I say? I would rather see you be a dancer? I would rather see you in a career where you might hold on until you're thirty-five if you don't get knocked out by a case of tendinitis or a bad knee?

"It's not an either-or thing," George said. "Just because I'm going to law school doesn't mean I won't still look great in tights."

"Sure," I said, trying not to sound defeated. "You can still dance."

And he did. He kept on teaching the level-three class on Saturday morning. George loved level three. That's where you start to re-learn everything you already thought you knew cold. He took the prima seventh graders through the six positions over and over again. George was a real stickler for detail.

But today was a Wednesday, not a Saturday, and this class wasn't a level at all. It was only the bumblebees, and there George was, dancing the role of the grandest daisy in the bunch.

"Aunt Taffy called," he said to me over his shoulder and then threw in a *grand jeté* just to show off for the girls.

"Roots in the ground, daisies," I said. "Use your arms."

"She wanted me to tell you she's on her way."

"She's leaving Atlanta now?"

George swung down from the waist, made a circle with his torso, and rose up again to the light. The girls followed him. I followed him. "No, no, no. She left at five o'clock this morning. She said she couldn't sleep, anyway. She said the house stank of Uncle Neddy."

I felt a little chill. "So where was she calling from?"

"She said she was right around the 40-85 split," George said in an ominous voice.

She was just outside of Durham. That gave me less than an hour if there was traffic, as little as forty minutes if the roads were clear.

"I tried to put the house together. Woodrow said he'd get one of the drywall guys to run the vacuum. He said he'd let her in, of course, if you didn't make it home in time."

"I can't just walk out of here." I clapped my hands. The girls looked up at me with

53

that expectant expression so often seen on the faces of puppies. "Now your roots come up, all the way out of the ground. That's right, now stretch up."

"I'll cover this."

"You have school."

"Believe me, it's easier to make up a day of law school than it is a day of dance class. I've read too far ahead, anyway. It's hardly even interesting." He turned his attention to the class. "Skip, daisies! Put your hearts into it! You're the first daisies on the planet who are able to skip!" George set off in a slow skip and the girls followed him. They would have followed him out of the school, down the street, and into the river.

"You're saving my life."

"I'm saving my own life. I don't want to have to listen to Taffy bemoan the fact that you weren't even there to meet her. Stretch your stems. Long daisy stems!" George pushed his shoulders down and made his neck into something elegant and the little girls strained to follow his example.

I told the girls I was leaving, but they hardly even blinked at the news. They loved me wildly unless George was around, and then they could barely remember who I was. Such is the fickle nature of the five-year-old. I was grateful to be able to leave without a sobbing daisy pulling at my ankles. It happens sometimes.

I wanted to stop off at the liquor store on the way home and buy the wine that Taffy liked, but all I could remember was that it was white and French and prohibitively expensive. I wasn't sure what kind of fruit she might want or what she ate for breakfast. As I tried to remember, I forgot that my sister drove me crazy, and instead gave myself over to feeling bad that we hadn't been closer over the years. We could make lists together. I would bring in whatever she wanted. I would buy flowers for her room and make sure the sheets were fresh. If there had been time, I would have cleaned the oven and rearranged the linen closet and turned over every cushion on every chair and vacuumed it. I was feeling the onset of a kind of nervousness that tended to manifest itself in weird and unnecessary cleaning. After all, my sister was getting divorced, my daughter was getting married. It was enough to make me want to put down new paper on the kitchen shelves.

chapter four

The vacuum needed to be replaced. It still managed to suck up a certain amount of dirt, but for the past year it had made, simultaneously, a horrible, high-pitched whine and a loud clacking that no amount of repair could get rid of. I could hear it before I even opened the door. There were no signs that my sister had arrived. It was only Woodrow and Kay sitting at the kitchen table, a stack of magazines between them.

"Who's vacuuming?" I said, raising my voice over the roaring that seemed to be coming from down the hall.

"Mr. Kelly," Woodrow said. Mr. Kelly was the plumber who had been brought over to assess how much pressure the crumbling foundation was putting on our pipes. "He's almost finished."

"George told me one of your guys was going to vacuum."

"Kevin was all set to go, he was plugged in and everything, but Mr. Kelly just took over. He says he loves to vacuum." Woodrow was practically having to scream. I hadn't thought about it before the vacuum was on, but he was a soft-spoken man. He waved me over to come and sit down at the table.

"I was showing Woodrow a few dresses," Kay said. She held up a picture in a magazine. It looked like a costume for *A Midsummer Night's Dream*, a blond nymphet tied up in panels of lace. There were a dozen different kinds of flowers woven into her hair. The dress seemed more appropriate for an ascension than for a marriage.

"I think she can go either way on the sleeves," Woodrow said.

"What do you think of sleeves?" my daughter asked me.

I didn't have a quick answer. I was still reviewing the questions: Why was someone who charged thirty dollars an hour for plumbing running my vacuum? Why was the contractor hashing out the issue of sleeves for a wedding dress that wasn't making an appearance for at least another six months? And, on behalf of my husband, why wasn't Kay at work? "Why aren't you at work?" I said.

"Markus Jones came in first thing this morning. It was like a miracle. I walked into the office and there he was, waiting for me. I ran him through his testimony, passed off some paperwork, picked up a stack of magazines, and here I am."

"Then help me get ready for Taffy."

Kay looked puzzled, almost hurt but not quite. "Don't you want to see which dresses I like?" She ran her finger over another page. The picture reminded me of Glinda the Good Witch in the scene where she shows up in Oz to tell Dorothy it's time to go home. It was a dress that cried out for a wand.

"Has the wedding been moved up? Are you getting married this weekend?" It was something about the sound of the vacuum. It made my nerves feel raw. Coupled with my impending company, I wasn't so interested in anyone else's problems. Suddenly Kay looked fifteen to me and I wanted to know why her room wasn't clean.

She slapped the pages closed. "If you're not interested."

"Taffy's going to be walking through the door" — I looked at my watch, hoping to say, In half an hour from now, but no such luck — "any minute. I'm going to need some help here."

"This is my *wedding*. This is the most important thing that's ever happened in my life. Would it be so terrible to sit down and talk to me about it for a minute? Woodrow was talking to me."

"I came in to get the paint cans," Woodrow said in his own defense. He pointed out the row of paint cans that lined my kitchen counters just in case I hadn't noticed them.

"I was going to put them out in the garage."

"Why does Taffy have to come now, anyway?" Kay's voice was a knot of petulance. "Can't you call and tell her this isn't a good time? We have so much planning to do."

"Not unless I call her on her cell phone as she's driving up the driveway."

"You don't even *like* Taffy. You like her even less than the rest of us do. I don't see why it would be so hard to tell her no." She leaned back in her chair and crossed her arms tightly over her chest. It was her way of saying that she was completely right and I was completely wrong. I know. I'd been watching her do it since she was three.

If I had been the kind of mother who recorded all the golden moments of her children's lives with a camcorder, I would take this opportunity to premiere the montage of Kay's finest moments. I would show what kind of person my daughter had been before the five-and-a-half-carat diamond was implanted on her left hand: Look, there is Kay at four, giving her bucket and shovel to the kid in the sandbox who doesn't have one. There is Kay at seven, reviving the starling that thunked itself cold against the living-room window (a lice-infested starling, mind you, not a cute little chickadee). There is Kay at every year of her life bringing home some animal that had been left mangled or abandoned by the side of the road. Kay at eleven giving all of her allowance to the Haitian relief fund after the priest's Sunday sermon about the suffering in Haiti. Kay at fourteen using her baby-sitting money to buy George the iguana that he wanted and I refused to pay for. Kay at thirty working in the public defender's office, for God's sake — what more proof did a person need than that? Is it possible that an engagement ring could change a person's brain chemistry?

"Listen," I said. "Give Taffy a break. She's having a very hard time right now." I wasn't being coy. I had every intention of telling them the nature of her hard time, but as soon as I said it, the vacuum was turned off and the doorbell rang and the three of us were suspended in a sudden void of silence.

"I'll get that," I said.

There stood my sister at the front door with a small red leather suitcase at her feet and a white wire-haired terrier named Stamp in her arms. Even though she had been the bane of my childhood, even though we had never been close as adults, my blood recognized her blood and I remembered what my mother worked tirelessly to drill into us: that a sister was a valuable thing to have in this world.

"Welcome home," I said.

"I look like hell," she said.

Taffy didn't know the first thing about

looking like hell. Despite having found out that her husband was leaving her yesterday, despite driving since the crack of dawn to get here, she was still nothing short of radiant. If the only thing Taffy had going for her was the hand that nature dealt her at birth, she would have been a beautiful woman. But she had more than that. She had taste. She had a personal trainer and a brilliant colorist she saw every six weeks. She had good jewelry, flashy Italian shoes, and a very, very subtle plastic surgeon of whom she did not speak. Because we had grown up in the same house, I knew that in a couple of weeks she would be turning sixty (she would swear to fifty-eight if anyone could get that much out of her), but time seemed to leave her alone. If she had been crying half the night, there would be no telling it. She looked like she was on her way to lunch at the polo club. She was wearing soft camel pants that matched her camel sweater set in silk, which matched the small brown ring around her dog's left eye. I leaned over to give her a hug, but her dog flashed his teeth at me and made a quick lunge in the general direction of my throat, which made me jump back.

"What's Stamp's problem?" I'd never particularly liked Stamp, but it wasn't as if we were strangers. He had no reason to want to take a piece out of me.

She put one hand over the dog's eyes to

make a temporary blindfold and then she gave me a quick kiss on the cheek. "Stamp is very protective of me if anyone gets too close. It's gotten worse as he's gotten older. I don't know how well he sees. He bites Neddy all the time now."

"Good boy, Stamp." I was glad to think that something in this life had bitten Neddy. It made me wish I had a box of biscuits.

"Everybody needs something that loves them best." Taffy gave Stamp a kiss on his forehead, leaving a little lipstick stain on his wiry white fur. "At twenty I was hoping for more than a dog, but at this point in my life a dog doesn't seem so bad."

I thought about Tom. I needed to call him. I leaned over and picked up the suitcase, which the dog didn't seem to mind at all. I guess he didn't feel protective about the luggage. Taffy put Stamp down and he immediately raced off into the house. A second later we heard a round of unrepentantly vicious barking. When I got to the kitchen, Kay was yelling at Stamp, who had stopped about six inches from Woodrow's shoes. Every bark was a small explosion that momentarily forced all four of the dog's feet off the floor. The bark was so high, so nerve-shattering, that I felt as if it was reprogramming the regular beating of my heart. Woodrow, on the other hand, never flinched, even though he was the one who was about to be swallowed whole by a twenty-pound fox terrier. He simply sat at the kitchen table and continued to drink his coffee, which in turn drove the dog to new levels of hysteria. Kay scooped Stamp up and, without thinking, tossed him out the back door, at which point he immediately charged at the four men who were unloading cement from a truck. In one balletic gesture the four leapt up and into the flatbed while the dog jumped up and up and up, every time almost reaching the back of the truck and every time crashing back into the driveway undeterred. The very hound from hell.

"Jesus," Kay said. "Why don't you keep that thing on a leash?"

Taffy seemed to be completely unaffected by the display and I had to wonder if it was a constant event at her house, if all across Atlanta the UPS men were drawing straws to see who would take the heinous job of delivering her packages. "No one keeps a dog on a leash inside. Besides, he's never bitten anyone except my husband. He looks like he's going to bite, but he never actually does."

"You should tell that to the men in the truck," Woodrow said.

"Is that yard completely fenced in?" Taffy asked. "I don't think I could take Stamp running off right now."

The chances of Stamp leaving that truck

were about as great as the earth disengaging from its orbit, but it was true, he needed to be relocated. Kay opened up the back door again. "Sorry," she said to the four grown men who were inching back toward the cab of the truck. "My aunt says it doesn't bite."

"Everyone says that," one of the men in the truck said. "And then after that they say, 'Look at that. You're the first person that dog's ever bitten.'"

Kay nodded and picked up the dog around the middle. She carried it with her arms stretched out in front of her as if it was something she was in a hurry to get into the wash. Stamp seemed to have no sense that he was off the ground. His legs still pulsed as if he were hopping. He barked at the men in the truck until Woodrow came into view, and then he barked at Woodrow again briefly until Kay took him down the hall, at which point he started barking at Mr. Kelly, who was just coming in with the vacuum. Mr. Kelly, a short, heavyset man in his fifties, pressed himself hard against the wall to give Kay and the dog as wide a passage as was possible. Kay opened the door to her old bedroom, where Taffy would be staying, pitched in the dog, and slammed the door.

"You don't have to throw him," Taffy said to Kay. "It works perfectly well to just set him down on the floor."

Kay was a lawyer. She was capable of controlling herself when she had to, but I could see the muscles working in her jaw, a gene she had picked up from her father. "Mr. Kelly, Mr. Woodrow, this is my aunt, Taffy Bishop from Atlanta."

"I thought that dog was from Atlanta," Woodrow said.

"Pleased to meet you, ma'am," Mr. Kelly said in a weak voice.

"Pleased to meet you," Woodrow said.

Taffy nodded at them and then turned to me. "Are you adding on to the house?"

"Well, that's how it started."

"I'm going to go on down to the basement and have a look at those pipes," Mr. Kelly said, taking a red bandanna out of his pocket and wiping down his large expanse of forehead. "That dog doesn't go down to the basement, does he?"

"Never," Taffy said.

Mr. Kelly left the vacuum in the middle of the hall and made a quick exit. He wanted to get away from us, all of us. He would clearly be more comfortable underground.

"I suppose I should be getting back to work myself," Woodrow said. He turned to Kay. He was hoping to calm her down. "We'll talk more about the dresses later. I just want you to be sure and pick something before I finish the job."

"Mother's right. We've got plenty of time."

Woodrow nodded and left the kitchen. He

65

was so tall and thin, so graceful that I always thought he could have been a dancer. He had once confided in me that even in his early sixties he was still plagued by people asking him if he had ever thought of playing professional basketball.

"The workmen are helping you pick out dresses?" Taffy said.

"It's not the workmen," Kay said, her voice breaking slightly. "It's Woodrow. Woodrow has very good taste."

"He has four daughters," I said. "He knows a lot about clothes."

"There's something here I'm not getting," Taffy said.

"Do you have more luggage?" Kay said. "I could go out and get it for you."

"Isn't George here? There's too much for you to carry in."

How much luggage could there be? "George isn't going to be home for a while. He's over at the school."

"He's at law school," Taffy said, not asking a question but telling me where he was.

"Actually, right this minute he's at the dance school."

"I'm getting the luggage," Kay said, clearly dying to leave the room. She was probably wishing that Markus Jones had never shown up this morning. She was wishing that she was still sitting in her office, tapping a pencil against her desk, waiting.

"Kay, be a dear and let Stamp out of the bedroom."

Kay detoured down the hall and we heard her kick open the door before disappearing outside. Stamp came back to his spot like a moth to a floodlight, parking it at the back door and resuming his barking as if he had never been gone at all.

"Is Kay having problems at work? I don't remember her having a temper like that."

"No, I think work is fine."

"Stamp," Taffy said, raising her voice over the drumbeat of dog bark. "Really, that's enough."

But what was enough for us was not enough for Stamp, who kept right on barking.

"Isn't George still in law school?"

"Of course he's still in law school. He just came down to cover my class for me so I could be here when you got in. To tell you the truth, I thought you'd be coming later."

"Minnie, I wish you wouldn't let George teach."

"Teach ballet?"

"It's not exactly encouraging him to go in the right direction."

"Which direction?"

Taffy shrugged. "You know I think the world of George. All I'm saying is that it's pretty clear that he could go either way, and ballet classes never steered any young man toward a normal family life."

"Are we talking about George being gay?" I had forgotten that Taffy had a penchant for speaking in code when the subject made her uncomfortable. "George isn't gay. Besides, this class is for four- and five-year-olds. It isn't a particularly corrupting level of dance."

"I still think it would be safer if he stuck to law school."

I wanted to explain that he was sticking to law school, but when I heard a thumping in the front hallway I went to help Kay wrestle in Taffy's suitcase. It was red leather, the same as the little bag I had carried in, but this one called to mind the kind of steamer trunks one took to Europe in the twenties if one was going to Europe for a year or two. Kay was sweating and her face was flushed, but she still looked calmer than she had when she left.

"How did you get that thing in the car?" I asked Taffy.

Kay slumped over the top of the suitcase and took a few deep breaths. "There's another one."

"I wasn't sure about what I'd need," Taffy said. "I was up in the middle of the night and I just kept putting more things in."

I thought about the way women in movies packed when they were leaving their husbands. They opened up a dresser drawer, scooped up the silky contents without looking at it, dropped it all into a suitcase, and then snapped the suitcase shut and made for the door, the feather-light bag in one hand. Taffy seemed to be operating on that principle, but she had clearly hit every drawer, every closet, in the house.

"Is Uncle Neddy coming up?" Kay said.

Taffy and I both looked at her. I remembered then that I hadn't told Kay about Neddy's junior executive. Last night wasn't the time, what with Trey and the ring, and there hadn't been a chance yet this morning.

"Neddy —" I said.

"Neddy left me," Taffy said. When she said it she turned away from us. I thought she was going to walk outside and collect herself for a minute, but instead she sat down on the floor in the front hallway as if all her packing and driving had suddenly caught up with her and she could not go another step. I was worried that there was drywall dust on the floor. As soon as she sat down, Stamp abandoned his post of growling and came trotting into the hall and climbed into my sister's lap. He made two full rotations on her soft camel pants, curled into a tight ball, and fell asleep. Then Taffy started to cry, and at the sight of those tears Kay began to cry, because Kay never could stand to see anyone else cry. She sat down on the floor and put her arms around Taffy. Stamp, perhaps exhausted by his long spate of ill temper, did not lift his head. They cried together on the floor, my daughter and my sister, until I was reduced to tears myself and slid down the wall to join them.

"I didn't know," Kay said.

I was glad that she didn't know because I think all of this crying made Taffy feel she had come to the right place after all. Taffy took Kay's hand and squeezed it, receiving the solid bite of the five-and-a-half-carat diamond for her troubles.

"My God," Taffy said. "You're engaged." She turned to me because I was the one who should have told her. "Why didn't you tell me Kay was engaged?"

"It only happened last night."

"Kay," Taffy said, her mascara starting to run, "I'm so happy for you."

That was as far as we had gotten, as much information as had been disclosed. We were three women sitting on the floor crying, with a suitcase the size of a Buick lodged halfway in and halfway out of the open front door. We were contemplating the institution of marriage, how it might fail or succeed, when Tom walked in and found us there. Stamp, startled from his sound sleep, woke up and bit him.

chapter five

Tom shook his leg. He gave three good kicks before the dog disengaged. As soon as Stamp no longer had his mouth full of my husband's calf, he started barking and growling as if he was thinking about going in for more. Who's to say he wouldn't have except for Kay getting her hand under the collar and holding him back.

"Look at that," Taffy said. "You're the first person that dog's ever bitten."

I scrambled up from the floor. "Are you okay?"

"Dad, are you all right?"

"Except for Neddy. He did bite Neddy."

"Jesus!" Tom leaned against the suitcase, holding one foot off the floor.

"Did he break the skin?" Kay said.

"I think he might have broken the bone." Tom winced and cupped one hand under his knee. "Did you train the dog to do that?"

"He never does that," Taffy said, clinging to the last thin strands of denial. Stamp was still racing toward Tom while Kay held him in place by his collar, his nails clacking ceaselessly to nowhere on the wood floor.

"You just said he bites Uncle Neddy," Kay said.

"That's entirely different."

"Has he had all of his shots?" I asked. I didn't want to think of Tom with rabies.

Taffy took the question as a complete affront to her competence as a pet owner. "What a thing to ask. Of course he's had his shots."

Stamp was barking like a maniac again. Kay tried holding his snout closed, but it wasn't possible.

"Kay, get your hand away from its mouth," Tom said.

"He's not going to bite Kay," Taffy said. "Stamp, stop it now."

Stamp ignored her. He kept on barking, scrambling forward to nowhere.

I knew it was up to me to look at Tom's leg. I was the wife. Somewhere in the marriage vows was an unspoken clause that you're the one who has to assess all bloody wounds. I wished that I could say that Tom was one to exaggerate injury, but he was a stoic. I'd seen him go to trial with a fever of a hundred and three and never issue a complaint.

I knelt back down. I held his shoe in my hand. There was a long, jagged tear in his suit pants (how he loved that suit, and it should have gone to Goodwill two years ago), and the edges were dark and wet. This wasn't going to be good. I found the indefatigable barking more wearing than the vacuum cleaner.

"How does it look?" Tom said.

"I'm not there yet."

"Taffy, if it isn't asking too much, maybe you could put Cujo here in the back? I don't want him getting excited by the sight of blood." Tom kept his eyes closed. He didn't raise his voice.

Taffy got off of the floor and picked Stamp up. Kay kept a hand on his collar until the last possible second. As soon as Taffy had him in her arms, he went limp, relaxed by his enormous output of energy. "You've got to remember he's a dog," Taffy said.

"I remember he's a dog," Tom said.

I was still holding his foot. I pulled back one edge of the torn pants like a curtain. There were two deep punctures, each jagged at the bottom where the dog had tried to hang on while Tom shook him off, each pumping a steady supply of blood into my husband's sock.

"This has been a traumatic time for him. Dogs have an excellent sense of what's going on around them. When you came in and startled him —"

"Taffy," Tom whispered.

"What?"

"Go put the dog in the back."

She sighed. Even if she had wanted to defend Stamp, she never would have won. Tom was a professional, after all.

"So, is this a trip to the hospital?" Tom asked.

"Oh, I'd think so. You haven't had a tetanus shot since you ran that piece of the gutter through your hand ten years ago."

"Do you think the dog had any rusty metal in its mouth?"

"Neddy never goes to the hospital," Kay said, making her voice sound uncannily like Taffy's.

"Ned pours a single-malt scotch into the holes and calls it a day," Tom said. "But I'm no Ned."

Kay wanted to come along and said she would call Trey and break their lunch date, but I talked her out of it. It was clear that Tom was going to live, and I didn't think there was any reason for all three of us to watch him get a tetanus shot. Besides, I wanted a minute alone with Tom. What with the impending marriage-divorce doubleheader, I had a feeling that time alone was going to be harder to get.

"Come back to work after lunch," Tom said to Kay.

"When you get to the hospital, tell them you don't know whether or not Stamp has rabies," Kay said, helping me walk Tom out to the car, one of us on each side. "Then the

Department of Animal Control will come and take him away. And you know if they take Stamp away, they'll have to take Aunt Taffy, too." She kissed her father and wished us luck, then she got into her own car and drove away.

"See if you can't get your leg up on the dashboard," I said to Tom. "I think you're supposed to elevate it."

The car was a little too small or Tom was a little too big. It took a good deal of effort for him to hoist his leg up onto the dash.

"So," Tom said. "Let's go back to my entrance, just before the part with the dog: I come into the house and I find the three of you on the floor crying."

"Oh, Taffy told Kay about the divorce and Kay told Taffy she was getting married. It was a little emotional."

"I thought you might have been crying over the size of her suitcase."

"It occurred to me."

"Tell me Stamp sleeps in the suitcase."

"I think Stamp sleeps in our bed and we sleep in the suitcase, but I'm just guessing. Why did you come home, anyway?"

"I called over to the school to talk to you, and George told me you'd gone home to meet Taffy. I'm not in court until after lunch, so I thought I'd come by, lend a little moral support."

"Lend a chunk of your leg." I turned down

the street that would take us to the hospital.

"Anything for the cause." Tom readjusted his knee into a better position. "It's not like I was bitten by a rottweiler. Do you really think we need to go?"

"Just for a minute."

Tom sighed. "To tell you the truth, I feel sorry for Taffy. You get to be this age, you think everything is pretty much settled. It would be a hell of a thing to have to rethink your whole life at this point."

I reached over the gearshift and took my husband's hand. I agreed with him. It would be a hell of a thing.

We were told that there would be no need for stitches, that puncture wounds needed to heal from the bottom rather than the top, a thought that made me feel squeamish. After the shot and a thoroughly unpleasant application of Betadine and antibiotic ointment, a bandage was applied and I drove Tom back to the courthouse. I thought we should at least go by the house so that he could get another suit, but he couldn't be late for court. "I'll put some tape on the inside," he said. "No one is going to be looking at my ankles."

"I look at your ankles all the time."

"Thank God Stamp didn't bite you. At least I can still work with a couple of holes in my leg."

"You'd sacrifice your leg for mine?"

"Any day."

It was the sign of a good man. "Call me when you're ready to come home."

Tom shook his head. "Kay can give me a ride."

I leaned over and kissed him. I tried to make it count. A person had to be diligent about kissing. Kissing was the affirmation of the union, the secret handshake that identified its members. And even knowing how important it was, it was easy to let it slide altogether, and suddenly one day you wake up and realize that it has been weeks since you've kissed your husband while you've had any clothes on. Worse still were the kisses that became mere gestures of kissing, those hard little pecks like the kind you got from a great-aunt when you were five, kisses that weren't kisses at all but said instead, I used to kiss you and this is the symbol that now stands in its place. It was the difference between eating a great meal and looking at a picture of food in a magazine: One made you feel full and the other only reminded you that you were hungry.

"I should get bitten by dogs more often," Tom said softly.

I kissed him again.

"What if the district attorney sees me making out in front of the courthouse?"

"He'll know he doesn't have a chance," I said.

Tom got out of the car, waved to me, and limped up the stone stairs, the bottom of his pants leg fluttering open in the afternoon breeze.

I felt a little guilty, using what had happened to Taffy to remind me that I was lucky for what I had, but I did it anyway.

The second I opened the door of the house, Stamp fired off like a handgun. It was a barking all out of proportion to the size of the dog. He sounded like a pack of police-trained Dobermans charging up the hall. You had to wonder where such a little dog was storing so much hostility. Taffy had wall-to-wall carpet in her house, and so when Stamp barreled up the oak floor to my front door doing ninety-five, he couldn't hold on to the turn and so skidded into the door of the coat closet, stunning himself for a second. Once he got on his feet again and saw that it was only me, he came over, sniffed my ankles benignly, and headed back to the kitchen.

"Is Tom all right?" Taffy said.

"I think he's fine." I dropped my purse on the kitchen table. I was still dressed from dance class this morning, which would save me having to change, since I had an afternoon class to teach in an hour.

"I think he overreacted a little. Neddy never goes to the hospital."

"He hadn't had a tetanus shot in years."

"Oh," Taffy said. "Then he needed to go anyway."

"He went because Stamp bit him."

"But Stamp really doesn't bite."

At the mention of his name, Stamp came over and sat on Taffy's feet with endearing loyalty. He looked like he wouldn't have bitten a squirrel if it was handed to him on a plate. The dog was more convincing than Brando. "The dog bites. The dog has bitten. You need to be more careful with the dog."

"Then it's just our husbands he bites. Nobody else."

"It isn't a decision you can make."

"You said yourself Stamp was a good dog for biting Neddy. How can he be good for biting my husband and bad for biting yours?"

"Because I love my husband." I didn't know if it was cruel of me to say, but it was true. "You may feel comforted by the fact that Stamp bit Neddy, but I don't want him biting Tom or anybody else around here. We've got the workmen to think of, and George will be home later."

"Stamp would never bite George."

George was a great favorite of Taffy's, even if she perceived him as teetering on the brink of homosexuality. "Listen, Taffy. I have a class to teach at three. I should get back over to the school pretty soon. Can we talk about this later?"

"What kind of class is it?"

"Mother-daughter tap."

Taffy looked wistful for a minute. "I should have taken tap with Holden."

"Were you ever able to find her?"

Taffy nodded. "I got her at four o'clock this morning. I forget what time it was in Cannes. Her secretary found her for me. She said she'd come home, but I told her not to. What could she do, really?"

"Maybe she could make you feel better."

"That's what you're doing. Or that's what you're supposed to be doing." She slapped her hands down flat on the table. "I'm going to come and take your class. I need to move around." As soon as she mentioned leaving, Stamp jumped into her lap and started to shiver like he'd been dropped into an ice bucket.

"My tap class?"

"Why not? I take Pilates and step aerobics. I should be able to tap."

Taffy in my classroom, taking my instructions? Taffy in a line of thirty-year-old mothers with their six-year-old daughters? "That wouldn't be any fun for you."

Taffy smiled. It was the first time she had smiled since she arrived. "What would be fun for me, exactly?"

Stamp began to whine and lick Taffy's neck. In truth, it would be good for her to come. There was nothing like concentrating on complicated footwork to take one's mind off of one's problems. Physical exhaustion was a good thing, and the thunder of tap shoes made it impossible to think. "Do you want to borrow something to wear?"

Taffy, whose combined suitcases contained more cubic feet of space than my entire closet, said she had everything she needed with her.

"You don't have tap shoes. Please, tell me you didn't pack a pair of tap shoes."

"Those I forgot."

"I'll get you a pair."

"Your feet are bigger than mine."

"Our feet are exactly the same size, you just wear smaller shoes than I do."

"You always stretched out my shoes."

"What? Forty-five years ago I stretched out a pair of your shoes? I'm going to get you some of my tap shoes. You'll see. They'll be fine."

"I can wear an extra pair of socks."

It didn't matter. It didn't matter if my feet were bigger or our feet were the same size and she needed to believe that my feet were bigger. It made no difference in the world, and still I had to swallow my overwhelming desire to tell her to take off her shoes, right here, right now, we were going to have a look. My sister's husband had left her. She was so lost that she was forced to turn up on my doorstep. I could find it within myself to keep my mouth shut. "I'll bring you an extra pair of socks."

"That would help." Taffy put Stamp on the floor and got up to go to her room to change. The dog kept leaping up and throwing himself against her as if he were still trying to sit in her lap even though the lap was no longer available.

"What about Stamp?" I said finally.

"I thought we could take him with us to the dance school." At the mention of this plan the little stub where I imagine there had once been a tail began to wag madly. There were certain concepts of language the dog had down cold.

"There is no way Stamp can come. The place is going to be full of children."

"Stamp likes children."

"I don't have insurance that covers dog-based liability. Don't you leave him alone in Atlanta?"

"We're not in Atlanta."

"Stamp can't come."

Taffy crouched down on the floor and took the dog's wiry muzzle between her hands. "She says you can't come, baby."

And with that devastating piece of information the dog slunk off and went under the bed.

"By the way, did you get your suitcases in?" It had just occurred to me that there was no longer a hulking piece of baggage in the front hallway.

"I asked the men outside. They said if I'd

82

lock Stamp in the bathroom, they'd bring in all of the luggage for me. The tall one, Mr. Woodrow? He said not to put all the bags on the same side of the room. He said your foundation is caving in."

George had held down the fort at the dance school all afternoon, but I didn't want him to miss criminal law. George loved criminal law. For someone who had never even thought of going to law school herself, what I knew about law school was not insignificant. Over the course of four children I had proofread papers, typed papers (but only in a real pinch — I wasn't much for typing), helped choose classes, and was endlessly asked to ask questions. *"San Antonio Independent School District* v. *Rodriguez,"* I said while making pancakes. "Charlie, get out the syrup. I'll get you started here, Supreme Court, 1973." And off they went. *"Kansas* v. *Hendricks.* Come on, this is such an easy one. Five-to-four vote upholding what lower-court decision? Think *Kansas.*" I prepped them, drilled them, and along the way I memorized a good part of it myself. And it wasn't just classroom experience I had, there were all the closing arguments I went through with Tom, too, all the heartfelt pleas for justice that I choreographed. For the thirty-odd years he'd been a public defender, Tom had stood at the foot of our bed in his pajamas, practicing what he would say the next morning. I told him when to look at the defendant and when to make an abrupt turn toward the jury box. Whenever I could manage it, I would go down to the courthouse to watch him. I loved to watch Tom in court. I always said he could have been a dancer. He said I could have been a lawyer.

Of all of my children, George seemed to be having the least problem with law school. I was never sure if he was smarter than the rest of us or if it was just that he had spent his entire childhood in an advanced prep class, always in the backseat of the car while the people in the front seat spoke in legalese. Other first-year law students complained of having to learn another language, but George was born fluent. He didn't ask me to drill him the way the others had, though from time to time we had conversations about cases. I think that they were more for my benefit than they were for his. I think that he just wanted to keep me up to speed.

When Taffy and I came into the studio, George was teaching three girls who had a private lesson on Wednesdays. In the wake of everything else that had happened, I had forgotten about them completely.

"Listen to the floor, ladies!" he called out. "It sounds like the elephants are landing! You could hear that landing in the six-dollar seats. I want this light, light, light." I was touched. It was the same speech I had been giving for years. George jumped straight up, did a brilliant full rotation in the air, and landed on the floor like a leaf on the lawn.

"Do you want to tell me it's completely normal for a boy to be able to do that?" Taffy said.

"I don't think it's normal," I said. "I think it's exceptional."

"*Port de bras,* ladies. You have arms and I want to see you use them. A little grace, please, a little extension." George stretched out his arm, turned his head, and saw us. He smiled, his face flushed and damp. He left the girls in arabesque and came over with his arms stretched out to Taffy. "My favorite aunt."

"Your only aunt," Taffy reminded him. It was true. Tom had no sisters.

"I'm sorry," George said before going in for the hug. "I smell like a sheep. But you, you look wonderful. You always look wonderful."

Taffy wore a black long-sleeved leotard, black tights, and my tap shoes with a pair of socks she didn't need. She had tied a jewel blue sarong around her waist that made the whole thing look smart, like maybe she was going to a dance class and maybe she was going out to dinner. "Now I know why I came here. All the McSwains know how to lie."

The three girls from the class slumped against the barre as soon as George turned his back on them. "On the floor, stretch it out," I said. "We've got another group coming in." The three of them sank down to the floor in full splits and pressed their bony chests toward the wood. Little ballerinas can be sullen, but they are endlessly obedient.

"That Katrina is a real swayback. You could set a cup of tea down on that girl's ass. You have to watch her every minute."

"I'll watch her," I said.

"Do you want me to do the tap?" George asked. "You don't have to stay."

"No," Taffy said.

"I'm sorry I left you here all afternoon. Taffy came in and then Stamp bit your father and we had to go to the hospital."

"Stamp doesn't bite," Taffy said, seeming to imply that perhaps I had bitten Tom and was trying to pin it on the dog.

"The hospital?"

"He's fine. He just needed a tetanus shot."

"Never a dull moment." George looked at the clock.

"Go to class," I said.

"Change clothes," Taffy said.

"There isn't time. If I run now I'll just make it." George gave us both a quick kiss and went flying for the door.

"You can't go to law school dressed like that!" Taffy said.

"They've already seen it all! We'll talk to-night," he called back to Taffy. "I want to hear everything."

But Taffy only waved. I don't think she particularly felt like telling everything to any of us.

chapter six

I am sixty-two years old and one of these days I'm going to have to buy myself a new left hip. Maybe, a couple of years after that, I'll need a right one, too. I will buy myself a set of dazzling plastic joints to replace the ones I've ground down over the years. I will reward my body with state-of-the-art technology, the very best that money can buy. It still surprises me that some mornings this body, which has been so strong and flexible that I could make a living off of it, lies in bed and doesn't want to go anywhere. But then it does. I stretch over one leg and then the other while I brush my teeth in the morning. I roll up onto the balls of my feet and stay there while I floss. It still works, it just takes a little longer to get it going. Tom will watch me down a couple of ibuprofen and suggest that maybe it's time to sell the school to Peggy, one of the teachers who works for me, who is saving up her money to buy it, but I'm not quite ready to let it go. And when the cars start driving up and the wave of little girls pours through the front door all decked out in their pink leotards and white tights, I know that I'll do this for as long as I possibly can. I never get tired of seeing them. Sometimes a few of the older ones will wear me out, but the little ones are my joy. Not every girl is going to grow up to be a dancer, and God, let us be thankful for that, but even the ones who will grow up to be physicists and heart-transplant surgeons are better off for having danced. Dancing puts you squarely inside your own skin. It teaches you that your body is yours, yours to move and bend and stretch. Dancing makes you listen to music with more than your ears and know that the music can be felt and applied. All of the little confidences of balance and grace, the pleasure of watching your own hand arc above your head in the mirror, the camaraderie of moving in a perfect line with others — I teach those things, and I like to think that somewhere the lesson lodges in the subconscious. I believe these girls are made better for having danced, even if it's only for a year. I believe that boys are made better for it, too, but in the forty years I've taught, I've probably had only two dozen boys come through my school. Maybe somewhere there's a football coach lamenting the lack of girls who signed up for practice in the fall.

Mother-daughter tap was started several years ago by a woman who would wait in the car and read while her daughter took class.

When the weather turned cold, she brought her book inside, and when she found she couldn't concentrate on her reading with all of those clattering shoes, she bought herself a pair of taps and took up a spot in the back of the room.

"They're six," I said at the time. "I think it's going to be a little slow for you."

She shrugged, a pretty young mother with brown hair and blue eyes. "I don't know a thing about dancing," she said. "I would never try to take a class with adults."

And so she danced. She danced pretty well but no better than her daughter. Soon the other girls told their mothers and the other mothers started coming with tap shoes of their own. It was all such a big success that I had to move the girls whose mothers didn't come into another class because they felt so horrible about the whole thing.

"God," Taffy whispered. "You forget how cute they are. And how little. Was Holden ever that size?"

"Probably so."

"I never wanted more than one child. I think that's because I always wanted to be an only child." She said it without any consideration of what that might have meant for me. "Now I think I should have had ten. Except not with Neddy. I should have had ten children born from illicit affairs."

I clapped my hands and the room went silent, all the mothers and daughters waiting and watching. It was better than being a lawyer. I was jury and judge, it was all my show. I put a record on and we started. "Has everyone been practicing?"

"Yes, Mrs. McSwan."

Taffy found an inconspicuous spot on the side of the room away from the mirror. She reminded me of that first mother who came to tap-dance. She was respectful but unself-conscious. Twelve little girls put their right foot out and tapped. Twelve mothers put their right foot out and tapped. Taffy put her right foot out and showed them all how it was done. They did a brush right forward, striking the pads of their big toes, and then a brush right back, brush right forward, brush right back. I called out the time but it looked for all the world like Taffy was leading them. They raised their rounded arms into third position a half beat behind her. Her steps were fluid, her tapping was impeccable.

Taffy could dance.

Had I known this before? She followed every step. She turned in the right direction every time we turned. She did not watch her feet. Not that it was hard, it was a kids' class, but it could be hard to do anything for the first time. This class had been going on for a while, and even the most uncoordinated children had memorized the routines. Taffy got them instantly. Her ankles were loose, her feet were quick. She knew how to work the top and bottom halves of her body together at the same time, a concept that some people are never able to grasp at all. It made me want to send the rest of the class home and throw routines at her all afternoon, real dance routines. I had a suspicion that she would be able to keep up.

"Let's do it slow the first time," I said to the class. "Shuffle ball change, shuffle ball change, then step ball change, step ball change. Good, perfect. Now speed it up, double time."

Taffy blinked her eyes and her feet started to fly. I could separate out her taps from all the other tap sounds because they were balanced, perfectly timed. Some of the children and mothers who had noticed a woman coming to class without a six-year-old were staring at her now, but they never would have put it together that we were sisters, Taffy with her chic blond hair in a swept-back cut, me with my brown hair gone impossibly gray and pinned to the back of my head like every other aging dance teacher I knew. Taffy in her careful makeup and me with a little Vaseline smeared over my lips. I was taller than my sister. She had a straighter nose, though that hadn't always been the case. I had taken good care of myself all my life, but I looked like what I was: a very fit sixty-two-year-old. Taffy, on the other hand, would soon be sixty and looked more like she would soon be fifty. It could be said that the only way anyone would have known we were related is that we were the two best dancers in the room.

"When did you learn how to dance?" I asked her as I waved good-bye at the window. The last of the little girls had come over to hug me, the last of the mothers had dropped off their checks for next month, we had the place to ourselves.

Taffy shrugged. "I always danced, I guess. Neddy was a terrible dancer. You couldn't get him out on the floor. I was always dancing with somebody else's husband at weddings."

"I'm not talking about that kind of dancing. I'm talking about this kind of dancing." I picked a little pink pullover up off the floor. There was always one left behind, no matter how many times I reminded them to take their things with them.

"I danced some."

"When? You hated to dance when we were kids."

Taffy leaned back against the barre and stretched her arms out to either side. "No, I didn't hate to dance, you loved to dance. There's a difference."

"You refused to go to dance class. Mother used to beg you."

"My refusing had nothing to do with my

not liking it. I didn't go because dance was your thing."

"What are you talking about?"

"It was always a competition with us."

"How could it have been a competition if you didn't even dance?"

"We were so competitive that we wouldn't even try to do the same things. I took some dance classes, but you were too far ahead of me. You were already too good at it and I couldn't win, so I quit."

"At six? You figured all of that out when you were six? That's not possible."

"It's not only possible, it's true." Taffy was relaxed, conversational. For her this was the friendliest exchange we had had in years. "We divided everything right down the middle: I was popular, you were smart. I jumped horses, you danced. I got Mother, you got Dad. If I was good in something, you never even went near it. If you were good at something, I gave it up."

"You got Mother, I got Dad?"

"It's true, isn't it?"

It was, but for the life of me I'd never thought of it that way. Little Henrietta, so named to be the son my father wanted, never interested my father a whit. I was the one who went to basketball games, who sat beneath his desk and read books when he had to go into the office and work on Saturday. Somehow I managed to be both a ballerina and the son he'd always wanted. For my mother, however, I was a colossal disappointment and my sister was the bright and shining star. "How did I miss that?"

"I have no idea." Taffy stretched up her arms and tapped out a little combination — hop left, flap right, flap left, flap right, shuffle left, shuffle right. She threw in a couple of double/triple-time steps. Without anyone else in the room, without the music, her feet made a beautiful, startling noise.

"So you took dance classes?"

"For a while, when I was in my forties. My therapist told me to. She said it was the only way to take back what you had stolen from me. Those were her words, not mine. I didn't actually think of it that way. But I liked the classes. I dropped them after a while — you know how it is. You get busy and then later on you pick up something else, water aerobics or something."

"How long did you take the classes?"

She shrugged. "On and off, about ten years."

"You danced for ten years? Why didn't you tell me?"

"Because I wasn't dancing. Not like you were dancing. I guess the therapist didn't solve the problem. I never thought she was very good anyway. Whenever I took a class, I just felt like I was trying to imitate you, and that was the last thing in the world I wanted to do. Anyway, who cares? This is all ancient history. I only came today because I was sure I had forgotten it all."

"Your feet betrayed you."

Taffy laughed. "First Neddy, then my feet. It makes me wonder what's coming next. Maybe Stamp will bite me."

"Never happen."

"Really, that would be the end."

"So you'll come back for another class, an adult class."

"I like the little girls."

"So come to both. Come to all of them. You can dance your heart out."

Taffy walked across the empty studio, her shoes clicking loudly with every step. My taps were off. I never could walk around in tap shoes. "What difference does it make now? I'm a little old to take up dancing."

I could see it all as if it were in front of me, Mother and Taffy heading out to shop, their hair curled, their sweaters matching, and I never cared because that meant I would be with my father, whose company I in every way preferred. "Everybody with any sense would like to be able to dance. It makes a difference because after Tom and the kids, there's nothing in my life that's made me as happy as dancing. I think dancing is just about the greatest thing in the world, so if I kept you away from that, even if I didn't know I was doing it, then I want to make that right."

"Oh, you knew you were doing it all right. And I knew when I was doing it to you."

"Fair enough," I said. We stepped outside into an early-evening drizzle and I locked the door behind us. "Fair enough."

We stopped off on the way home and picked up Chinese. I felt guilty about not making dinner on Taffy's first night in town, but it was already too late to start cooking. When we got back to the house, our arms full of take-out bags, Woodrow was sitting at the kitchen table with Stamp lying on the floor near his feet. Stamp was attached to a leash, the handle of which was tied around one of the legs of the table. When we came in the door, he sat up and barked once but Woodrow held out his hand.

"Ah," he said. Stamp put his head back on the floor and whined, the stump of a tail beating time against the floor. He was desperate to jump on Taffy.

"Why is Stamp tied up?" Taffy said.

"Because he tried to bite me," Woodrow said.

I put down the Chinese food and rubbed my eyes. I had forgotten to shut the bedroom door. "Oh, God, Woodrow. I'm sorry." I gave Stamp a sharp look but he only wagged.

"He didn't bite me," Woodrow said. "He tried but did not succeed."

"See," Taffy said, bending down in front of her dog. "He doesn't bite."

"Oh, he bites. He bit Kevin who does the drywall. That's why we're having a little training session."

"Is Kevin all right?" Maybe I was lucky to be in a family of lawyers. I pictured lots of lawsuits during Taffy's visit.

"He's fine. Stamp here only tore up his jeans."

Taffy rubbed Stamp's ears. Woodrow asked her politely to stop. "He's thinking about how it's best not to bite people right now. He needs to focus on that."

"You can't just train another person's dog," Taffy said.

"I can if he's biting the men on my crew. We're in and out of this house all day. We can't do that if there's a dangerous dog here, and if we leave the job, then, your sister's living room is going to wind up in her basement pretty soon."

"Don't leave. Don't even talk about leaving." Woodrow was gone too much as it was. I believed that my house was unraveling and that he was the only thing that was holding it together. Without Woodrow our property value would be equal to a box of toothpicks. Every day new cracks were showing up in corners.

"Do you know how to train dogs?" Taffy stood up and stepped back from Stamp. He started to cry, but Woodrow put up his hand and said, "Ah," again.

"My father trained dogs. It was my brother who took over the business, but I got a good look at what was going on. My father had dogs that could work math problems and serve coffee. They were the smartest, best-behaved dogs you ever saw in your life."

"Stamp had a trainer when he was a puppy," Taffy said hesitantly. "But he didn't take to the classes. My nutritionist told me that some dogs can have attention deficit disorder."

"I'm sure that's true," Woodrow said. "But fortunately, that's not the case with Stamp, here. Stamp has no problem paying attention once you explain the rules to him."

About that time Tom and Kay walked in and Stamp lunged forward with such purpose that the whole table jerked forward a couple of inches. A sharp ridge of hair shot up on his back and he flashed his teeth. Tom stepped back into the hallway, pulling Kay along with him. Woodrow stood up.

"Ah!" he said sharply.

Stamp lay back down again, but he kept his eyes on Tom.

"You didn't hit Stamp while we were gone?" Taffy said suspiciously.

"I certainly hope somebody did," Tom said, leaning cautiously back into the kitchen.

"There's no way he can get out of his collar, is there?"

"There is no call to hit a dog," Woodrow said. "You never hit anything that's beneath you. That's what my father always said."

"Well, my father always said, Never bite the man who's letting you sleep in the guest room," Kay said.

I gave Tom a considerably less meaningful kiss. "How are you feeling?"

"I'm fine. Just a little sore."

"Well, sit down for a while. I'll get you a scotch and you can pour it on your leg if you want to."

Tom went to sit down at the kitchen table, but Stamp started growling again. Woodrow got up and shortened the leash by several inches so that there was no way the dog could get anywhere near Tom.

"That can't be comfortable for him," Taffy said. "He isn't used to being confined."

"You can put him in the bedroom if you want, but he needs to learn to be around people without biting them. This is the only way he's going to learn it."

Very tentatively, Tom sat down at the opposite end of the table from Stamp and put his leg up on a chair. We all watched the dog to see what would happen next.

"I don't mean to be rude," Kay said. "But may we stop talking about Stamp for five minutes?"

"It's a good point. All this attention doesn't help things, either. Kay" — Woodrow stood up and pulled out a chair for her — "come sit down here and tell me more about those wedding dresses you were looking at this morning."

"Actually," Kay said, hoisting her briefcase onto the table, "Mrs. Bennett came by the office this afternoon and dropped off some sample invitations."

"I didn't get to meet her?" Tom said.

"You were in court," Kay said. "We stood in the back and watched you for a minute but she needed to get going."

"She has sample wedding invitations lying around?" This particular point seemed stranger to me than her not meeting Tom.

"They were from Trey's sister's wedding last year. She bought the sample book because she said you never know when you're going to need that sort of thing." Kay pulled out stacks of creamy off-white cards in giant envelopes. Everything about the paper said *important document*. It was the kind of paper that should have been used for the Magna Carta, the Declaration of Independence, the marriage of the eldest Bennett son.

Taffy came over and ran one finger over the engraving. "This is very nice."

"Mrs. Bennett — Lila, she wants me to call her Lila, but I don't think I can — Mrs. Bennett said it wasn't too early to start thinking about these sorts of things."

"Why can't you call her Lila?" Tom said. I handed him a drink and he accepted it with gratitude.

Woodrow picked up the stack of cards and started going through them. He was holding them with his arm straight out and squinting at them, so I took my glasses off my head and handed them to him. "Oh, that's better," he said.

"Are you the contractor, dog trainer, wedding consultant?" Taffy asked him. Her tone was neither kind nor unkind. She just wanted to know.

"Woodrow has gotten three of his four girls married," Kay said. "And he made most of the arrangements himself. He has a lot of experience with weddings."

"But more experience with dogs." Woodrow looked at each invitation carefully and then divided them into piles. "I've had many more dogs in my life than I ever had daughters."

"What about your wife? Didn't she help to plan the weddings?"

Woodrow smiled and put the cards down. "My wife died when the girls were still in school. That's why I wanted the weddings to be especially nice. I wanted them to be the kind of weddings they would have had if their mother had still been alive."

"Oh," Taffy said, looking down at the envelopes. "Of course."

"I'm going to put out some dinner," I said, wanting to change the subject. "Everything is casual. Woodrow, you'll stay for dinner?"

Woodrow nodded. "I live here, don't I?"

Suddenly, Stamp was barking again and the table was hopping across the room behind him like an oversized dogsled. Woodrow got halfway out of his seat and Stamp lay down and whined.

"It looks like somebody's been a very bad dog," George said as he came into the kitchen. Clearly, he had never gotten around to changing clothes after dance class. He was wearing sneakers, a leather jacket, and his tights. He looked like James Dean trying out for *Swan Lake*.

"You're just in time for dinner," I said. I had raised four children, three boys, and I knew how to buy food. I bought lots of it, more than I could ever imagine needing, because in the end somebody always ate it. You never knew who was going to show up and how many people they'd have with them. George had not come home alone. He'd brought Jack with him, or, as he was commonly known at our house, Jack from the D.A.'s office.

"My timing is perfect," George said.

"Jack," Kay said.

"Jack," George said. "Of course you know my parents. This is Woodrow, who is rebuilding the house, and this is my aunt,

Taffy. I ran into Jack on my way home."

"The D.A.'s office is on your way home?" Tom said.

George didn't appear to be listening. "I told him Kay was getting married and he wanted to come and congratulate her. Now he can stay for dinner. Jack didn't know that Kay was getting married."

"It only happened last night," Kay said. I thought she looked a little pale.

But Jack didn't seem pale at all. If George was trying to shake up his sister, then Jack was on his side all the way. He walked right up to Kay and kissed her forehead. "This is wonderful news," he said. Then he picked up her hand and whistled. It was a very sincere whistle. "Now, that says Engagement."

"I haven't seen the ring," George said. He took his sister's hand away from Jack and held it up. "What is this? He asked you to marry him and he gave you a flashlight?"

"Stop it," Kay said through her teeth.

"So you've set the date?" Jack said.

Kay shook her head. "This only just happened."

"But you have the invitations already."

"Samples," Kay said. Her voice was weak.

Jack picked one up and looked inside the envelope as if it might contain something illegal. He sniffed it. "I'll be the first one in the church. I always like to get a seat on the aisle so I can see the bride."

Even though the D.A.s and the P.D.s were on opposite sides of the fence, they were all county employees and they had the look of county employees, which is to say that Jack looked like a guy who slept in his suit. I could see about two inches of tie coming out of his coat pocket. He needed a shave. It was a look I found endearing since I had spent a long time looking at it on Tom.

"I imagine it will be a big wedding," Jack said.

"Oh, pretty big," Kay said. She didn't seem interested in talking about sleeves or invitations anymore. She looked very much like someone who wanted to go back to the office and do paperwork until four in the morning.

"How big?" Jack said. "I know it's early but, ballpark, what are we talking about here?"

"I'm not sure," Kay said.

"But if your future mother-in-law dropped off the invitations, she must have mentioned a figure to you," Taffy said, picking up on the line of questioning.

"Even a very rough figure," Jack said.

Taffy picked up one of the envelopes. "How many people were at her daughter's wedding last year?"

Kay waited for a minute as if she were trying to tally up a list of names in her head and come up with a number. "Maybe six hundred."

"Six hundred people?" Tom said.

"Maybe a few more than that."

I felt my hand clutch the counter. Six hundred bread-and-butter plates? Six hundred place cards? Six hundred slices of cake? Was that even possible? Who knew six hundred people?

"I'm starving," George said. "Should we go ahead and eat?"

chapter seven

And so it was dinner for seven: Taffy, my
sister, whose husband had left her; Kay, my
daughter, who was marrying Trey Bennett;
Jack from the D.A.'s office, who was sleeping
with Kay; George, my son, who had brought
Jack over to torment Kay; Woodrow, the wid-
owed contractor who was trying to save our
house; Tom, my husband, who had two
puncture wounds in his right calf from my
sister's dog, Stamp, who was tied beneath the
table; and me. Seven. There was room for all
of us. There was even an extra chair so Tom
could keep his leg up. There were so many
white paper cartons on the table that
someone who was just dropping in might
have thought that we were in the business of
manufacturing them. We were used to having
this many people for dinner, but this exact
combination was a new one for everybody.

"I think I'd like a drink," Kay said. "Does
anybody else want some wine?"

Jack raised his hand.

"Red," she said.

"Just bring it all to the table," I said.

Kay came back with two bottles of white and two of red. The corkscrew was stuck into the waistband of her skirt and she immediately devoted herself to the business of getting all of the bottles open.

"White," Taffy said. Tom handed her a bottle. She filled her glass up to the top and then filled up Woodrow's glass without asking him if he wanted any. "This is nice, the big kitchen, the big kitchen table. Mother always said that eating in the kitchen was strictly for the help, but I think that it's very charming."

"That's why I always eat in the kitchen," Woodrow said. "At least when I'm here."

"Taffy, that's awful. Did Mother really say that?"

"It was something like that. Neddy and I always made a point of eating in the dining room, but then half the time he didn't make it home for dinner. I thought I needed to have some consistency, so when he was off working, or doing God knows what, I'd eat in the dining room by myself. It's a huge room."

"The most wasted space in a house," Woodrow said. "When people are building, I always tell them to cut back on the dining room. At least you made an effort to use your dining room."

"I only use my dining room for addressing our Christmas cards," I said, which was an exaggeration but not too far from the truth.

"Now you can use it for addressing the wedding invitations," Jack said.

"They pay someone to do that," George said.

"Stop it," Kay said.

"Do you build houses?" Taffy asked.

"We build some houses. We do renovations, repairs. I like to think we can do whatever needs to be done."

"What's going on here, anyway? There's all this work, but I can't really tell what's happening."

"Six hundred people," Jack said.

"Maybe a few more than that," George reminded him.

"I shouldn't have said anything," Kay said. "I have no idea really."

"Is that the chicken with garlic sauce?"

Tom looked inside a couple of the containers and then he passed me the chicken with garlic sauce. "Kay's got a big trial coming up."

"What's the case?" I asked. There was a time when I would have known. There was a time when Kay would have told me who she was defending and who she was thinking about marrying.

"I don't even want to think about it," Kay said. "There's so much that's going to need to be done, and then I try to think of that case —"

"If you need any help, I'd be happy to run

up some background for you," Jack said, heaping a pile of shrimp fried rice onto his plate.

"Best we don't let the D.A.'s office take over our cases," Tom said. "Not that we don't appreciate the offer."

"Just want to be helpful," Jack said brightly.

"The drainage system in the original house wasn't installed properly. For all these years some of the water from every rain has been running under the basement. After a while everything just starts to crumble. Are those the egg rolls?"

Taffy handed Woodrow the egg rolls and a couple of plastic packets of bright red sauce. "So the house is rotting?"

Jack took a steamed pork dumpling under the table and gave it to Stamp, but Woodrow missed it. I was quite sure that feeding Chinese food to the dog under the table wasn't part of his training program.

"Some of the supports have rotted. It's amazing to me, really, that the whole thing held up this long."

"Is it safe to be in the house?" Taffy took a long drink and looked around the table. "I mean, there are so many people in the room."

I leaned forward. I was interested in this one.

"We've put in temporary supports. The

house is safe enough for now."

"The contractor said 'safe enough,'" George said. "Think how that's going to sound in court when our dinner guests start to sue."

"I hate to ask this," Tom said, catching half the conversation to his left, "but how much longer do you think it's going to take?"

"Counting the Florida room?"

"Sure," Tom said. "Counting the Florida room."

Woodrow pressed his lips together and leaned his head to one side. He was clearly going over some invisible list, but he couldn't seem to reach any conclusion.

"It's okay," Tom said. "I shouldn't have asked."

"A lot of it depends on getting these other jobs finished up."

"I kind of hope it doesn't get finished until I graduate from law school," George said. "I've gotten so used to Woodrow and everybody being around."

"Law school's only two more years," I said.

"He asked me to dinner," Jack said. "Would you have rather I said no?"

"Well, you didn't have to say yes."

"I've been coming over here since we were in law school. Now you're getting married and I'm not supposed to see your family anymore?"

"You have a family," Kay said.

"They always liked you," Jack said.

"At least you have someone around who can fix things. If our living room had fallen into the basement, Neddy wouldn't have noticed. I swear to you he didn't know how to plug in the toaster."

When the wine came around for the second time, I went for the red even though I had started with white. I didn't want to wait for the white.

"What kind of work does your husband do?" Woodrow asked Taffy.

"He's in the soft-drink business, I guess you'd say. Or he was when I left him this morning." Taffy followed my lead and refilled her glass with red.

"What happened with Uncle Neddy?" George asked.

"Neddy found himself a junior executive."

Sweet George, who I wanted to kill for bringing Jack to dinner, reached over the table and picked up my sister's hand. "I always thought Uncle Neddy was an idiot," he whispered.

"I'll second that," Woodrow said. "And I've never even met the man."

Taffy teared up a bit in the face of kindness. "Neddy was an idiot," she said softly.

"So what about wedding presents?" Jack said. "Have you given any thought to what you want?"

"You know perfectly well I don't want a

wedding present," Kay said. Her voice was choked and I thought she might be following Taffy's lead and getting a little misty.

"You don't want wedding presents from anyone or you don't want one from me?"

"Does this seem to be going south?" Tom whispered to me, one sweet-and-sour shrimp held aloft on his fork.

"That would imply that at some point it had been going well," I said. We drank. The Chinese food performed a sort of miracle: The more we ate, the more there seemed to be.

"Tell me something about your wife," Taffy said to Woodrow.

The doorbell rang. Stamp snapped the red leather leash taut and growled. Woodrow went under the table to speak to him.

"I'll get that!" Kay said.

She wasn't fast enough. I was already out of my chair. I was, possibly, even more desperate to walk out of the room for a minute than she was. I hoped that a pack of Christian missionaries would be waiting on the porch, all of them looking to save my soul. I planned to invite them in, get them each a plate of Chinese food. I would listen to them all night.

But when I opened the door, there was no one there to make me a true believer. It was Trey, the Bennett, the bridegroom, my future son-in-law. He was wearing a navy suit and a navy-and-yellow-striped tie. He was carrying a bunch of pink spray roses tied up in clear cellophane with a pink silk ribbon. It was a scene from a movie: You open the door and there is a handsome man with his handsome bouquet of flowers. The suit was handmade in Milan, the flowers had just been taken off the plane from Amsterdam. Every tiny rose was in perfect bloom. For an instant I wondered if he was stopping by to show me the very pinnacle of possibility for the spray rose.

"Trey," I said. "Kay will love those." I could hear the trace of complete wonderment in my own voice.

"They aren't for Kay," he said, and extended his full hand out to me. "They're for you."

I should have said no. I should have said, Kay's having a hard night, go in and give them to her, but instead I reached for those flowers as if I was drawn in by their light. "They're beautiful."

"I'm sorry that we were so late coming by last night. I let my mother take things over sometimes. It wasn't very thoughtful of me."

I looked at the roses. There were as many as seventy, and each one could fit inside a thimble. Was it possible to even buy flowers like these in Raleigh? Without dipping my face into the bouquet, I could smell their rosy sweetness. "I'm leaving you out on the porch," I said. "Come in, come inside. We're having dinner. It's just Chinese food." I said a prayer. If there is a God in heaven, please let Trey say that he's already eaten. "Have you eaten?"

"I had something brought up at the office."

I gave the credit to the Christian missionaries in my imagination. "Well, come in and say hello. My sister is here from Atlanta, Kay's aunt."

Trey and I walked into the kitchen. The flowers had made me dreamy. For a moment I had lost sight of what I had left behind. Except it was worse now. Taffy was crying. She wasn't crying hard and she was managing to more or less hold her eyeliner in place with a paper napkin, but it didn't look good. George had his arm around her shoulder. Kay and Jack had their heads down and were bickering in low tones. Tom and Woodrow were both looking around the room for the emergency exit.

Stamp gave a short growl but didn't bark at Trey, and for that Woodrow went down on the floor again to praise him.

"Look at those flowers," Taffy said. "You look like you just won the pageant."

Kay raised her head to look at the flowers. She had forgotten that the doorbell had ever rung. "Trey."

"Trey?" Jack said.

"Trey Bennett." Trey offered his hand to Jack and Jack rose up to take it. It wasn't the kind of scene that any woman enjoyed watching. Kay came out of her chair slowly and Trey kissed her.

"Jack and I went to law school together," Kay said to Trey by way of explanation.

"But we're on opposite sides now," Jack said. He'd had a real spark in him all night, but suddenly it had gone out. He was no longer teasing Kay about getting married, now he was meeting the man she was going to marry and that was nowhere near the fun. He looked like the rest of us, someone who would rather be someplace else. "I'm at the D.A.'s office."

"I'm always so glad to meet a friend of Kay's," Trey said.

The rest of the introductions were made. Taffy balled the damp napkin up into her left hand and extended her right hand to Trey. Maybe it had been a bad dinner, maybe we were falling apart, but it was good to know that we could still rally ourselves to our best manners when the occasion arose. Tom's leg was stiff from having been up and he hobbled a bit when he went to fix Trey a drink, but he was smiling, grateful for an excuse to leave the table. While he was up he got out a vase and put my roses in some water.

"I've stayed so late," Woodrow said, but it wasn't even seven o'clock yet. We had started dinner very early.

"I don't mean to break up the party," Trey said.

Woodrow patted Trey on the shoulder. "Don't you think that for a minute. I got here at six-thirty this morning."

"Woodrow has a life of his own," Tom said, and handed Trey a glass of cranberry juice with ice.

"Could you give me a ride?" Jack said. "I came over here with George."

"I'll take you back," George said.

But Woodrow said that he was going that way, even before Jack told him which way it was. They said their good nights and Woodrow gave Stamp a long scratch on the back of the neck and let him out to the full length of his leash. "He wants to be a good dog," Woodrow told Taffy, and then we all said good night.

Tom started picking up plates, but I told him to go into the living room with Trey for a while. I think he would have rather walked around with the dog hanging off of his leg than try to make any more conversation for the evening, but he and Trey went out to sit with Taffy. George and Kay helped me pick up the plates.

"I'm thinking about killing you," Kay said to her brother.

"He's a nice guy. What were you going to do, let him read about it in the paper?"

Kay started stacking up plates. "Whatever I

was going to do, it was my decision, all right?"

"I'll clean up," George said. "Go on in the living room and hang out with your fiancé."

But then Kay put her plates back down on the table and started to cry.

"Oh, God, Kay," George said. The sight of Kay's tears threw every member of our family into a panic. "Listen, I'm sorry."

"George," I said. "Go into the living room. We'll finish this." I wanted to find a way to head this crying off at the pass. It wouldn't be long before Trey would wander back out to the kitchen and then he'd want to know what Kay was so upset about. If she was to give in to the bout of weeping, there would be no stopping it.

George looked helpless and utterly guilty, but I sent him away. Kay and I hadn't had a minute alone since she had come in the night before to announce her engagement.

"Do you want to talk about this?"

She put her hands over her eyes and shook her head, but then after a minute of taking deep breaths, she reversed her decision and nodded. "I want to marry Trey," she said.

"That's a good start," I said. "What about Jack?"

Kay went over and shut the kitchen door, which was never, never shut. Then she tore a paper towel off the roll and blew her nose.

"Jack is Jack. Jack is never going to get married."

"And if Jack had wanted to get married, would you have married Jack?"

She sat down on the floor next to Stamp and unhooked him from his leash. For this act of kindness he crawled into her lap and licked her neck. "What I wanted was something simple, something really clear and straightforward like what happened with you and Dad. I always imagined that one day somebody was just going to ask me to marry him and that it was all going to make perfect sense. And then Trey asked and it felt so great. Trey is a great guy."

"You don't marry someone because they're a great guy, you marry them because you love them, because you can't imagine spending the rest of your life without them."

"I know all of that," Kay said, rubbing the dog's ears. She had forgotten that she had been mad at him. He was a dog, after all. "But who's ever really sure? Say a client tells me he's innocent — sometimes I really believe him, sometimes I'm almost positive, but how do you know? I mean, were you sure? When you and Dad got married, were you positive that you loved him and you couldn't ever really love anybody else?"

I put down my plates and sat on the floor with Kay and Stamp. I tried to think back, not to remember the funny story we told but to try to remember the day itself, who I actually was then when Tom sat in the lobby of my dormitory and asked me to marry him. My parents still sent me spending money every month. I had a picture of Anthony Perkins pinned up inside my closet door and liked nothing better than to stare at his sad, delicate face. I had never voted. My concept of time was divided into semesters. Was I sure about love, that this was the person I would be eating my meals with and raising children with and making love to for so many years? I had no idea. I wanted to tell my daughter that I had been absolutely certain, but I think what I had been is absolutely lucky. I don't think that I knew Tom's middle name when I married him. It didn't matter. We had been full of a dreamy sort of romance then. Maybe we had excellent intuition about each other, but the real love came later. I think, probably, the real love always comes later.

"It was such a long time ago," I said. A truly feeble answer, but what was I supposed to say? That marriage is a cliff dive? That you can do all the research you want, but you're never really going to know if it's going to work or not until you jump? That hardly smacked of sound maternal advice. Instead I said what a mother should say: "But if you aren't sure, you don't have to make the decision now. You've got plenty of time."

Kay shook her head. "I'm thirty years old. I want to have children. There's a wonderful guy in the living room who wants to marry me and who I am almost entirely sure I love. I don't think it's going to get much better than that."

"Thirty is nothing," I said. "It's just the start."

"That's not what you would have said when you were thirty." Kay mopped up the last of her tears and combed out her hair with her fingers. "I'm going in there," she said. "Do I look all right?"

That night when Tom and I went to bed I asked him, "When you asked me to marry you, were you sure about it?"

"Sure, I was sure about it. Why? Did Kay say she wasn't sure?"

The room was dark. I propped up on one elbow and looked at what little I could see of my husband's head on his pillow. I had been looking at him for more than two-thirds of my life. In the bad light, with my glasses off, he was exactly the boy I had married. Tom at twenty-three was in bed next to me, wanting to get some sleep. "Let's forget about Kay for one minute."

"I can do that."

"When you asked me to marry you, was it because you were sure I was the person you wanted to spend the rest of your life with?"

"I guess I must have been if I asked you."

I had lived too long with lawyers to accept that as an answer. "Come on now and think about this for a minute. I'm serious. Why did you ask me to marry you?"

Tom sighed and closed his eyes. I knew exactly what he was thinking: His daughter was getting married, his sister-in-law had moved in, his house was falling down, he'd been bitten by a dog, and now his wife wanted to know why they had gotten married. It was too much for a Wednesday. "We had had that fight."

"The fight no one can remember."

Tom was quiet for a minute. "I remember it."

"Are you serious? All these years we've told the kids we couldn't remember and you knew? What was the fight about?"

"Basketball."

"We broke up over basketball?"

"I had promised to take you out to dinner for your birthday, but then at the last minute I got tickets to the Duke-Alabama game and so I told you I was sick."

And there it was, the missing piece of the story, the least important element: the fight that had been obliterated by its own outcome. Once prompted, I could half remember it: I had made some sort of soup. Chicken soup. I made the noodles myself in the kitchen of a friend who had an apartment. I spent my birthday making noodles and soup, and when I took it over to Tom's, his roommate told me he had gone to the game. At the time I'm certain I had been furious, but now it seemed funny. "Why didn't you ever tell me you remembered?"

"Why do you think? It didn't come up for ten years, and when it finally did, I was thrilled that you had forgotten. I'd done something stupid and you had the decency to forget it."

"So why did you want to marry me?"

Tom mulled over the question in the dark. Maybe he hadn't thought about it in forty-two years, or maybe he had never thought about it, but the answer was a long time coming. "It was the soup, I think," he said finally. "You had left me the soup even though you knew I wasn't sick and I had lied to you. When I went over to talk to you that night, you said you could never date a person who lied and that was that. I went back to my dorm and I ate the soup. It was so wonderful. I kept thinking, Where am I ever going to find another girl who would spend her birthday making me soup when she thought I was sick? Where am I going to find a girl who would still give me the soup even though she knew I was a lying creep? The more soup I ate, the worse I felt about the whole thing."

"You married me because the soup was good?"

"I asked you to marry me because after the fight I missed you. I figured if I missed you that much then you must be the person I was supposed to marry."

"But that's not the same as being completely sure."

"Well, that depends. Is being sure you don't want to be apart from someone the same thing as being sure you want to be with them?"

"It's probably close enough."

Tom slid one arm under my waist and pulled me to him and pulled himself over to me. I put my head on his chest and listened to his heart. It had been the single most consistent sound in my life. "Do you want to tell me what's stirred all this up?"

"You were right. It was Kay. She wants to know how a person is supposed to be sure about who they marry."

"First you find someone who knows how to dance." Tom rubbed my hip, the little knot that was always there. He found it and untied it. "Then you wait to see if they bring you soup."

I kissed him and then broke away to pull my nightgown over my head. I dropped it on the floor and then I kissed him again. "And if they bring you soup?"

"Marry that person immediately."

124

chapter eight

Three days later Lila Bennett called and invited me to lunch. I immediately regretted not having made the preemptive strike. We should have invited the Bennetts out to dinner, then the four of us could have met together. Tom and I could have touched our shoes under the table in the reassuring way we did in certain social situations. We could have dissected the evening in the car on the way home and made something funny out of it no matter how badly things might have gone. But it was all too late for that. She had asked and there was nothing to do but to go. I was on my own.

"Shouldn't we invite Tom and Scout?" I had asked hopefully on the phone. It was Sport. Sport. Scout was the little girl in *To Kill a Mockingbird.*

"Just the mothers this time," she had said to me, graciously ignoring my gaff. "There's so much work to be done."

"Well, you can't wear any of this," Taffy said, sliding my clothing piece by piece down the bar in the closet while I sat on the bed.

"Oh, come on, there has to be something in there."

She held up my favorite black blazer, tilted her head to one side. "I don't think so."

I was a fairly secure person, but I knew that fashion wasn't my strong point. I tended to favor clothes that could be worn over other clothes. "What about the dark purple dress?"

Taffy laughed and closed the closet door. "Forget this. Come with me." She waved me down the hall and I followed her to her room, sat down on her bed, Kay's bed. How many times had I sat on this bed while Kay dug through her closet trying to decide what to wear on a date? "Why do I have three brothers?" she would wail. "I need somebody I can borrow clothes from." She never thought of my clothes as a possibility, either.

But I had never worn my sister's clothes. Growing up in the same house, it never would have occurred to either one of us to borrow something from the other one. Our sense of style was defined by our direct opposition to each other. Now there was a rain of featherlight cashmere sweaters falling all around me. Stamp jumped up on the bed and made himself comfortable in a red cardigan. Stamp was only allowed off the leash when he was in Taffy's bedroom with the door closed.

"Woodrow said Stamp wasn't supposed to

be on the furniture," I said.

"Not true," Taffy said. "He is allowed to get on my bed. I already told Woodrow, I sleep with Stamp. There's no point in even having a small dog if you can't sleep with it."

"Did he sleep with you and Neddy?"

Taffy just looked at me. Stamp looked at me. Of course they all slept together.

She looked at a beautiful navy dress with a scoop neck and then put it back. Then she pulled out a gray pantsuit made out of some kind of soft knit. She held that one up for a while and I started feeling hopeful, but then she shook her head. She went back into the closet. "Here we go. This is nice. This would be good on you." Taffy pulled out a green suit that was neither drab nor bright but the rich color of a holly leaf. She held it in front of her and looked in the mirror. "This is your color," she said to her reflection.

"Do you think?"

"Trust me."

"I'm taller than you are."

She tossed the suit on my lap. "You are two inches taller than I am, maybe less. That doesn't mean that you can't wear my clothes."

I touched the fabric. It was a wool gabardine as light as silk. It was gorgeous. Why in the world did she think to bring clothes like this with her in the first place? Maybe we should start taking her out more. Taffy shuffled through her closet for a blouse. "Shouldn't I be myself? If Kay and Trey get married, we're going to be seeing these people. Sooner or later she's going to know what I really look like."

"First impressions." Taffy held up a blouse that at first I thought was off-white but on closer inspection I could see was ever so slightly peach. "This gives you power. You're going to need power. Take your clothes off."

Taffy had been notoriously modest when we were young. Not only did she refuse to change clothes unless the door of her room was bolted shut, she would scream if anyone else tried to change clothes in front of her. As I pulled my sweater over my head, it occurred to me that I hadn't seen her naked since she was seven years old. "We never did this," I said, picking up her blouse. It slipped over my arms like a breeze. I caught the name of an impossibly famous and expensive Italian designer before I buttoned up.

"Did what?"

"Tried on each other's clothes."

"I'm not trying on your clothes."

"You wore my tap shoes."

She thought about this and nodded. "True enough. Still, it would have been hard to imagine doing something like this when we were young."

I stepped into the skirt and zipped it up. "It's shorter than what I usually wear."

"That's because most of your skirts hit your ankles. How can a person who spends half her day wearing a leotard be modest? You worked hard for those legs. You should show them off." She draped a scarf around my neck and then helped me on with the jacket. I looked like the chairman of the board, the extremely stylish, slightly sexy chairman of the board. "Shoes," she said.

"I have shoes."

"I refuse to let you wear that suit with flats." She went back to the closet.

"I've always found high heels to be uncomfortable."

Taffy stared at me. "Do you think that is specific to you?"

"We don't have the same size feet," I reminded her.

"Shut up," she said kindly, and handed me a pair of heels.

I looked in the mirror. From the neck up I was still myself, but from the neck down I had never looked better. "I love it. I will live in fear of spilling something on it, but won't I be seriously overdressed for lunch?" I slipped on the shoes and felt my hip shift forward.

"You won't even be in the ballpark of overdressed." Taffy took a step back, gave me a look of hard assessment, and then smiled. She took the heavy gold hoops off her ears and handed them to me. They were warm.

"When she asks you where you got the suit, and she will, do not say your sister's closet. Say, Atlanta."

"Atlanta," I told Lila Bennett. "I was visiting my sister."

"They have the best shopping in Atlanta." Lila Bennett ordered us each a glass of white wine and handed the menus back to the waiter.

"Yes," I said dimly. I was thanking God for Taffy because if I had been wearing my purple dress at this moment, I would have had to excuse myself, go to the rest room, and try to climb out of a window. I had been to the restaurant before, though I'll admit not knowing they served lunch. The hostess said, "Welcome, Mrs. Bennett." The waiter said, "It's always good to see you, Mrs. Bennett." Even the busboy nodded to her as he spooned the star-shaped pats of butter onto our plates. I would not have said that Lila Bennett was beautiful or homely or heavy or thin. All I could say was that she looked like money, extremely subtle, extremely old money. Everything about her was tastefully elegant, expensively compiled — her jewelry, her hair, her manicure. Wearing the nicest outfit that I had probably ever had on, I was just breaking even.

"I should tell you right away, of course, that we simply adore Kay."

Again I was scooped. "We think the world of Trey."

"And we couldn't be more pleased about the wedding."

I was absolutely going to say that. Dammit. Salads arrived. Suddenly I felt unsure of my fork. This was insanity. I was a perfectly well-mannered person. I wondered how Kay managed whole dinners, entire long evenings at the Bennetts'. I wondered how Trey had managed it for a lifetime. "We're very happy," I parroted back. Why hadn't I insisted the four of us get together, husbands and wives? Why didn't I think to demand that Kay and Trey be included as well? I had spent my life dancing in front of strangers, and now I couldn't eat a salad or navigate the simplest patterns of conversation?

"I think they should wait a year." Mrs. Bennett gently pierced a bit of endive but did not bring it to her lips. "I know they're in such a rush, no one can wait for anything these days, but what they forget is that it takes so much planning. It would be simply impossible to manage it in six months, even if we all work together. I have a woman, Mrs. Carlson, who is a wedding planner. She did my daughter's wedding. Mary Hunt's wedding was only six hundred people, maybe a few more, and we spent a year on that."

"Only six hundred?"

"A few more."

I picked up my glass. When the wine arrived, my original thought had been that it would be better not to drink, but now I could see that wouldn't be possible. "And how many people are you thinking about for this wedding?"

"Trey's?" she asked, making sure we hadn't moved on to a discussion about some other wedding.

I nodded, sipped.

Mrs. Bennett (and I will make a point to explain to Tom why Kay can't imagine calling her Lila) tilted her head. "I think a thousand would be the cap. I'd like to see nine hundred, but these things never turn out exactly the way you think they're going to. But that's just me guessing at your list. I don't know your numbers at all."

"Fifty?" I offered.

She nodded. "So then it would be nine hundred or a thousand."

I drove around the corner to a gas station and called Tom from a pay phone. I did not chat up Alison, his secretary. I told her to put me through. "Can you meet me in the parking lot?" I said.

"What's wrong?"

An old man with seven teeth and an oily rag in his pocket smiled at me. It must have been my suit. "I need to talk to you."

"Can't you come into the office?"

132

"I don't want to run into Kay. Just come outside. I'll be there in five minutes."

When Tom got into the car, I was trying very hard not to perspire. I had one arm propped up on the window and the other one draped over the back of the passenger seat. He kissed me with some enthusiasm.

"You look fantastic," he said. "Where did you get that outfit?"

"It's Taffy's," I said flatly. "It all goes back to the closet this afternoon."

Then he remembered where I had been. "This is about lunch," he said.

"That's right."

"This is not good news about lunch, either."

"Right again."

Tom stared out the window and exhaled. He didn't pressure me. Whatever I was going to say, he was in no hurry to hear it.

"Lila Bennett is thinking a thousand people, maybe nine hundred. She pointed out that traditionally the bride's family pays for the wedding, but given that their guest list was so much larger — she was very tactful about all of this — given the enormity of their guest list, she thought it would be fair to split the whole thing down the middle. With them paying for the rehearsal dinner, of course. They would insist on paying for the rehearsal dinner."

Tom continued to stare. I wasn't entirely sure he had heard me. We both sat in silence while cars shot past us on the street. I wondered if we could run away. I wondered if Tom knew someone who could get us into the witness protection program. Wasn't there a branch of the witness protection program that was for parents who couldn't pay for their daughter's wedding?

Finally Tom's head dropped forward onto his chest as if his neck had just spontaneously snapped. It was very startling. "I'm not going to be able to retire," he said.

"You're not going to be able to retire? Do you think that's the answer to this? You're going to have to join a corporate law firm and make full partner in the next six months if you want to pay for this thing."

"What are we going to do?"

I looked at the heavy gold bracelet Taffy had lent me. Pawning that would be a start. Maybe I could pawn the suit, too. "Realistically, we have two options: We assume a level of debt that would crush us until our death if we were able to borrow that much money in the first place, or we tell Kay and the Bennetts the truth: We simply can't do this."

"Maybe we could offer to pay a smaller percentage."

"It's possible. But what if the wedding costs a million dollars? Do we offer to pay ten percent?" The image I had of us standing on the coast of the Mediterranean vanished, or, I should say, the sea was still there, but Tom and I had been excised from the picture. We had put all four of our children through college. We hadn't paid for anyone to go to law school, but all four times we had helped. It had not been easy. It had taken a lot of planning and creative financing. We weren't living on the edge, but the edge was in plain sight. We had saved up for the Florida room, but we still didn't have a Florida room. Having the bottom of our house rebuilt had shaken us up some, and now to think that after a lifetime of work we could be finished off by one large party, wiped out over cake and a dress, we were stunned. "It's my fault," I said. "I should have just told her no. I should have said it straight out the second she brought the whole thing up."

Tom blinked. "I might be able to get us a spot in the witness protection program."

I will say it: I have never felt closer to another human being in my life. I told my husband how much I loved him.

He reached over and held my hand and we sat there, two married people in the life raft of their car.

"How was the suit?" Taffy asked. She and Woodrow were sitting in the kitchen eating their own late lunch, with Stamp tied to a table leg between them. He growled at me and wagged his tail at the same time, which seemed like progress.

I sat down and took off the earrings and the bracelet and put them out on the table so as to return them before my baser instincts got the better of me. "The suit was a big success."

"It's a great suit," Woodrow said.

"It's mine," Taffy said. "Did she ask you where you got it?"

I nodded.

"I knew it. I knew she would ask."

"What's wrong?" Woodrow asked. "You don't look so good."

"What are you talking about?" Taffy said. "She looks gorgeous."

"No," Woodrow said. "Look at her."

And that was all it took. I put my elbows on the table, my face in my hands, and I cried.

"My God," Taffy said. "What happened at lunch?"

I told them everything and they both listened carefully.

"You can't do what you can't do," Woodrow said. "There's no sense torturing yourself over it. Pick up the phone right now and call her."

Taffy shook her head. "Wait awhile. It's a big decision. You need to think it over.

You're not going to pay half, but you need to look at what you can pay."

"These people have more money than some countries," Woodrow said. "Why should she have to pay anything?"

"If it were one of your girls, you wouldn't want the other family taking care of everything," Taffy said to Woodrow. "Just because somebody has more than you doesn't mean that you have no responsibility. Think about Kay. How is she going to feel if you don't even make an effort?"

"Will she feel so different if we offer to pay five percent?" I said. What did Taffy know, anyway? Her daughter wasn't married, and when she got married, she and Neddy would have all the money in the world to spend. Holden had plenty of her own money, as far as that was concerned, and she tended to date movie stars, who weren't the kind of people who expected the bride's parents to pay for the wedding anyway.

"Maybe I was wrong," Woodrow said, his voice sounding disillusioned. "Maybe this business of marrying rich people isn't as great as I thought it was."

I thought about Jack the D.A. in his rumpled suit and scuffed shoes. He was probably the kind of guy who would talk a girl into going to Vegas. He'd want to be married by an Elvis impersonator with hired witnesses you had to tip later. And God bless him for it.

I had a class to teach at three o'clock, though my head was so full of numbers I didn't know how I'd ever make sense out of music.

"Ah-ah," Taffy said when I went to get behind the wheel. "Give me the keys, I'll drive."

"It would be different if I were completely convinced that Kay wanted to marry him in the first place."

"How would it be different? You'd have more money?"

"No, I'm just saying, it's one thing to destroy your entire financial future if you know they're going to stay together and be happy, but to destroy it and then have the marriage fall apart . . . I think that would kill me."

"Oh, who the hell knows? When I married Neddy I thought I was the luckiest girl in the world. I'm getting divorced now, but if someone had suggested it to me then I would have socked them in the jaw. I was absolutely sure that there was nobody else for me, and I guess, if I was going to be perfectly honest, for a while it was true."

"You loved Neddy?" I don't know why this surprised me.

"Sure I loved him."

"Do you love him now?"

Taffy cut across two lanes of traffic and got in the left-hand turn lane. Taffy was a dynamite driver, I would give her that. "You spend all those years with somebody, how do you know? Do you love them now or is it just that you used to love them? Is it that you get into patterns — How did you sleep? How was your day? What sounds good for dinner? It has something to do with love, but I don't know what, exactly. All I'm saying is, if Mother and Dad were still alive, I don't think they'd be entitled to a rebate on my wedding. I think even though things didn't work out in the end, I got their money's worth out of it."

Taffy pulled up in front of McSwan's. "I really don't think I can do this," I said.

"You can do this," she said. "You always do."

But I wasn't doing it well. The class was Tap One, which came after the Bumblebees and Introductory Tap. These were seven- and eight-year-olds and they had a keen eye for mistakes.

"Mrs. McSwan! You keep saying, Shuffle shuffle *flap* ball change, but you keep doing shuffle shuffle *step* ball change."

I looked at my feet. What were my feet doing? They could fly on autopilot. I should be able to do this stuff when I'm dead. I tapped my toes together and stood there feeling utterly lost. Then suddenly the seas were parted and a leader stepped forward.

"Okay now, girls," Taffy said. "I'm Mrs. McSwan's sister. I'm the other tap teacher."

"You're Mrs. McSwan, too?" asked a suspicious eight-year-old with a fat red braid.

"For now, yes." Taffy clapped her hands. "Get in line, girls, because we've got work to do." She rattled off a routine: "Starting on the right, flap, flap, flap, heel, heel, pick up heel, toe, heel, shuffle heel, cramp roll, and then repeat." It was nothing they knew. It was more complicated than what they were used to. Taffy accepted no mistakes. I went to the side of the room and watched for a change. She made them go over it again and again. In the end, they all got it.

That night Kay called. "I talked to Mrs. Bennett," she said. "She just loves you."

"She loves me?"

"She talked a lot about your posture. She said you were very elegant. She said she wishes she had been taking dance classes all these years."

"Well, I guess it's never too late to start."

"Are you all right?"

"Sure I'm all right, why?"

"I don't know. I guess you just sound tired."

"It was a long day."

"Well," Kay said. "I really just wanted to call and thank you."

"For going to lunch?"

"I know that sounds crazy, but she can be a little overwhelming."

"I was happy to do it. I wanted to." I waited for a minute. I wasn't sure if I should ask her at all. Maybe I should wait and ask her when my voice wasn't shaking. "Kay, you know all those things we were talking about in the kitchen the other night?"

"Don't worry about that. I was just being emotional. Seeing Jack threw me off course for a minute, but I'm fine now."

"So you're feeling better . . . about marrying Trey?"

"I feel great about it," she said. "I think this is going to be the best thing that's ever happened to me."

"That's great. That's all I wanted to know. But if anything changes, you'll tell me?"

"Of course I'll tell you," Kay said, her voice reminding me of the little girl she had once been. "I tell you everything."

Tom and I lay in bed in the dark, my shoulder pressed against his shoulder.

"Is that a crack in the ceiling?" he said.

Maybe. Maybe it was just a shadow. "I can't tell. It's too dark."

"I'm going to turn the light on for a minute."

I grabbed his arm. If there was a new crack in the ceiling, I absolutely did not want to know about it until morning. "Don't you dare."

He settled back down next to me and let

out a sigh. I think he was relieved that I had stopped him. "What are we going to do about all of this?" he said.

"I don't know. I feel like my brain is spinning. I can't even think anymore. All I know is that we shouldn't turn the light on."

Now we were both staring at the ceiling, wondering if it was slowly splitting in half.

"Did you ever think about getting a divorce?" I asked him.

"Divorcing you?"

"Unless you were married to somebody else."

He waited a beat. "Maybe," he said, "just for a minute when it's pouring down rain and I realize you've taken the umbrella out of the car again."

"I'm serious."

"I'm serious, too." We were quiet for a while. We watched the ceiling. "Did you ever think about divorcing me?"

I had and he knew it. There had been a time. The boys were seven and nine, Kay was almost five. Things had been going along okay and then one day Tom and I were like two people who had never even met before. I don't know what happened. Everything that passed between us took the most unbelievable amount of effort. Every conversation, every arrangement, even handing him a cup of coffee in the morning felt nearly impossible. It was as if we had wandered into a darkness that we couldn't find our way out of, and at the time I had thought, This is it. This is over. The word *divorce* set up camp in my brain. But then one day we woke up and we could see a little bit of light and we just kept moving toward it. Just as fast as things had gone bad, we turned another corner and found our way out. Who knows how these things work? When we came out of that slump, it was like we had found each other again. I was so happy. There was a long period of giddiness, and it was in that time that we wound up with George. I don't know why we fell apart or how we fell back together, but after that we were always more careful with each other. We taught ourselves to be kinder, more patient. We had seen what we stood to lose and it scared the hell out of us.

There was moonlight coming in through the window now and it might have been enough to see the ceiling, but I didn't look in that direction. I looked at my husband. "No," I said, kissing the curve of his neck. "I'd never divorce you."

chapter nine

Four days later, Stamp was off the leash.
Woodrow had brought over a little dog bed
for him that was kept beneath the kitchen
table, and on the morning of his liberation,
Tom and I came into the kitchen and didn't
even notice that anything had changed.
Woodrow had made the coffee and was
reading the paper before descending into the
basement. There was no barking, no
growling. As soon as we sat down, Stamp got
out of bed and walked over to sniff Tom's
leg. Tom put down his coffee and looked
under the table.

"It's all right," Woodrow said. "He's just
checking things out."

When Stamp was finished surveying whatever damage he had done to Tom, he came
over to me and I scratched his head. Then he
lay down on the floor beside Woodrow's feet.

"What did you do to the dog?" Tom said.

"I just gave him a few boundaries. Everybody needs boundaries."

"So is he finished?" Tom asked. "Is this a
reliable dog?"

Woodrow looked at Stamp, who seemed to know we were talking about him and began to thump his stumpy tail without opening his eyes. "I would hope that Stamp would stay around for a while. He is a better dog, but I wouldn't call him reliable quite yet."

Tom suggested that maybe he could finish up with a correspondence course from Atlanta.

Woodrow nodded and picked up the paper again. "It's possible. But it takes so long to teach them to read."

If Stamp stayed, Taffy stayed. Or maybe it was the other way around. She took her empty suitcases across the hall to Henry and Charlie's room and stored them there. I did not ask her how long she planned to live in Kay's old bedroom and she did not volunteer the information. After the first week had passed, all she would say was that she thought that Stamp was learning a great deal and that she was looking on the whole experience as a kind of dog college. "Maybe this is what was supposed to come out of my marriage," she said. "Maybe Neddy was supposed to leave me so that I could come up here and Stamp could get some help. Woodrow said that the first step was for me to admit that Stamp needed help."

"You don't actually believe that, do you?"

"God, Minnie, have a sense of humor."

Most nights Neddy called.

"Car-o-line-a," Neddy said, putting the original *a* back on the end of my name so as to get out the full four syllables. Neddy loved syllables. It was how he had always said my name. I had never particularly liked it, but now that he was planning to extricate himself from the family, it seemed almost unbearable to the ear.

"Ned."

"How are things going up there in Raleigh, North Car-o-line-a?"

"Is there something you need, Ned?"

"I was calling to speak to Taffy, but I'm always glad to have the chance to talk to my favorite sister-in-law." Fave-or-right.

Did he think I didn't know? I suppose it was possible that he thought Taffy wouldn't tell me and that I would assume that this was simply the first long visit of our lives. The complete nondisclosure of personal information would have been in keeping with our relationship up until this point. "I'll get her," I said, and dropped the phone onto the table.

Whenever Neddy called, I reminded Taffy that she was under no obligation to come to the phone and that I would be more than happy to lie to him on her behalf, but she always shrugged me off. She came into the kitchen and picked up the receiver.

"Hmm?" she said, and spread out her fingers to study the coat of polish she had just finished applying. She pressed the phone between her shoulder and her ear and listened. From time to time she rolled her eyes. "Um-hmm. Right." She blew on her fingers. "Third drawer in the bathroom. No, on your side." She waited. "Your side. Well, look again. No, I didn't take them. No. Go look." She waited for a minute and then looked up at me. I'll admit it, I found the whole thing strangely fascinating. "I'm on hold," she said.

"You have hold in your house?"

Taffy nodded and then held up her hand. Ned was back on the line. "There. Exactly. What did I tell you?" She waited. "That's right. Okay. Okay, bye." She hung up the phone and shook her head in disgust. "He thought I had taken his toenail clippers. As if I have ever used toenail clippers in my life."

"Why do you tell him where they are? Why do you even talk to him?" Every night Neddy called looking for the extra set of car keys or wanting to know if there was something in the freezer he could eat for dinner. Sometimes he'd call back five minutes later asking how he was supposed to heat it up. Taffy always told him.

"Why isn't the junior executive finding the toenail clippers?"

"I told him she wasn't allowed in the house. Anyway, Neddy hasn't mentioned her again."

"Why don't you ask him? You don't seem

to talk about the divorce or what's going to happen."

"It's too depressing."

"So why talk to him at all?"

"He doesn't know where anything is."

"So what? Why shouldn't he have to look for things?"

Taffy didn't like to talk about Neddy. The subject made her weepy and she hated to cry about as much as most fully dressed adults hated to be thrown into swimming pools, but she took a deep breath and tried to explain it to me in terms I could understand. "You always had a job," she said patiently. "You had the studio. You had four kids and the house and Tom to look after. Well, my job was to take care of Neddy. He was always adamant that we hire people to help with Holden because he didn't want anything to distract me from my job, even if it was our daughter. And I went right along with it because I figured that's just the way things were." She stopped for a minute. I must have been staring at her with blank disbelief, so she tried again. "What would you do if someone came in and told you you weren't allowed to teach dance anymore? Wouldn't you have days when you still felt like you were supposed to go to work? If the studio called and asked you how to turn on the heat and where the tax records were kept, wouldn't you tell them?"

"Not if they tossed me out on the street after a lifetime of loyal service."

"Well, all that means is that you're smarter than I am, and we've both always known that."

But I didn't know any such thing. Childhood is the time to cobble together an identity: I am good at this, I could never do that. I love this, I wouldn't touch that. We put together lists, stake claims. The people around us make assumptions and we grow to fit them. I can remember my mother sitting on the edge of Taffy's bed at night, combing my sister's long blond hair and twisting it into pin curls, Taffy sleeping with her head full of pins without complaint, and then in the morning my mother would take out all the bobby pins and carefully brush her hair. Never was there a child with more beautiful hair, heavy yellow ringlets that came halfway down her back. People would come up in the grocery store and ask if they could touch Taffy's hair. But I couldn't stand to sit still. When my mother rolled up my hair, it became a battle of wills. The more I jerked around, the more likely she was to poke me with the pins and so the more I complained. I felt like I was sleeping with a head full of nettles, and in the morning when the whole thing came down, my hair was still no competition for the silky cloud that fell over my sister's shoulders. So I said I didn't like to have my hair curled. I said that it hurt and that it was a waste of time, which meant there was no place for me in the evening ritual that was now just between my mother and Taffy. I went downstairs and pretended I was interested in watching the news with my father, until finally I was interested. Taffy was praised for her beauty and received pink smocked dresses for her birthday. I was praised for being smart and got a set of *The Children's Encyclopedia of Knowledge*. I read the books, Taffy wore the dresses, and inch by inch our worlds moved farther apart.

I'm sure the decisions we make about ourselves at six and eight and ten are helpful, but do we still have to live with them at sixty and sixty-two? If Neddy had been my sister's life's work, then it was time for her to get another job. The second week that Taffy was with us, I told her to come and work for me.

"That's the stupidest thing I've ever heard."

"I'm not saying you should teach point classes, just teach the Intro to Tap. Teach Tap One. Teach the Bumblebees if you want to. It's a room full of five-year-olds. You like the five-year-olds."

"I don't know how to teach."

"I saw you teach. You were great. You've danced every day you've been here. You know you can do this."

"Don't you have to be licensed?"

"You're not teaching them how to fly."

"Woodrow told me I should get a job," she said.

"Woodrow?"

"He said I was going to go out of my mind if I just kept sitting around. I told him if that was the case, I would have gone out of my mind a long time ago."

"What does he think you should do?"

"He thought I should learn how to train dogs."

"Why? Because you did such a good job with the one you have?"

"Woodrow says I have a great rapport with Stamp."

"He's only saying that because he hasn't seen you dance."

Taffy stalled. She seemed like the most coolly self-confident person in the world, but the idea of teaching rattled her. "I don't even live here. I'm going to go back to Atlanta eventually."

"I won't make you sign a contract. I won't even pay you. I'll put your salary in the wedding fund."

"There's a wedding fund?" George said. He came in and went straight for the refrigerator. "If Kay has a wedding fund, then it's only fair that I get one, too. There needs to be some equality in this family."

"I'm trying to talk your aunt into teaching

151

a couple of dance classes," I said.

George took a bite of an apple and chewed it thoughtfully. "Well, it would certainly get the piano off my back. If you're covering classes, it would mean that I wouldn't have to run down there every time somebody caught a cold."

"You'd quit teaching?" Taffy said to George. "You'd want to do that?"

"I am in law school," he said. "I know that law school is very passé around here, but I do have a lot of work to do. I need to get through a hundred pages of reading this weekend for Torts alone." Then George glanced out the window and his face froze. His mouth was still open and I could see little bits of apple sitting on his tongue.

"Are you choking?" Taffy asked.

"Who is that?" George said.

I turned around and looked out the window. "That's Erica."

"Who's Erica?" He put the apple down on the counter and walked to the window.

"Woodrow's daughter."

Erica was wearing blue jeans and a green plaid shirt with the sleeves rolled back. She was getting a shovel out of the back of the truck. When she turned around and saw that all of us were staring at her, she gave a big wave, and headed off to work. Clearly, Erica was a girl who was used to having people stare at her.

"There are four daughters," George said weakly.

"This is the one that's still at home," I said. It was funny. I had never seen George like this.

"You're telling me she's been here before?"

"She works with Woodrow sometimes on Saturday."

"Then why haven't I seen her?" Erica went out of view and George walked over to the other side of the table and craned his neck.

"Have a little dignity," Taffy said.

"You're never home on Saturdays," I reminded him.

"What does she do?"

"She's in nursing school."

"Why didn't anybody mention this to me before? Woodrow never said a thing to me." He looked at me and pointed his finger. "You never said a thing to me."

"It's rude to point," I said, pushing his finger aside. "And Woodrow mentioned Erica not two weeks ago. You just weren't listening." I put down my coffee and went to the back door. "Erica, could you come here a minute?"

Erica smiled. I hadn't really thought about it before, but it was a fairly dazzling smile. She leaned her shovel up against the truck. Her father was already down in the basement. "You haven't met my sister and my son."

"Oh, hey," she said, holding out her hand to Taffy. "I've heard so many nice things about you. My dad talks about you all the time."

"He does?" Taffy said.

"Oh, it's Caroline's sister this and Caroline's sister that. And this must be Stamp."

We had all forgotten about Stamp. He had been completely silent when Erica came in, but now he rolled over on his back and let her scratch his belly. "What a good dog you are," she said.

George waited his turn.

"This is my son George," I said.

Erica stood up and wiped her hand on her shirt. "Excuse me, I have dog hands now. Hello, George," she said, and smiled again.

At that moment, if she had said, George, I think we should get in that truck and drive to California for lunch, he would have gone. "Hello," George said.

She might have stayed longer, but George didn't come up with anything after hello. "Well, it was great to meet you both. Thanks for calling me in. I should get back to work, though. I'm on the clock."

"Do you need some help?" George said.

"Working?" Erica said.

"I could carry your shovels downstairs or something. I mean, I live here. I should at least try to help."

Erica laughed and shrugged her shoulders.

"Sure," she said, "if you want to." They were walking out the door when Erica stopped and turned around. "I'm sorry," she said. "I just realized that I don't know your name."

"Taffy Bishop."

"Taffy," Erica said, and smiled again. "Isn't that funny that Dad always calls you Caroline's sister?" She waved and then the two of them went off to the truck.

Taffy looked out the window and then looked at me. "Well," she said.

"Well, what?"

"Well, she's —" She didn't say the word *black*, she only mouthed it.

"Either he teaches at the dance studio and winds up gay or he goes out with Erica Woodrow," I said. "Take your pick."

Through the window we watched Erica pick up the shovel again, but George took it away from her. He was talking and talking and pretty soon he put the shovel back into the truck. Erica looked like she was listening, but it was impossible to tell by the expression on her face whether or not she liked what she was hearing.

"Can you tell what he's saying?" Taffy asked.

"No idea."

George lifted his hands. He put his feet in fifth position and then went up on his toes. Erica started laughing.

"Looks like he's trying to impress her," I said.

"Are you kidding me?"

"Really, I think George has amazing luck with this."

Woodrow came up the basement stairs. When he saw what was going on he came over and stood with us. Stamp whined a little bit until Woodrow reached down and rubbed his ears, but soon he was looking out the window again. It was as if we were watching a flock of especially dazzling birds who had landed on the feeder, streaks of sunlight reflecting off of bright blue feathers. "What is this about?" he asked.

"Court and spark," I said.

"Is he supposed to be dancing?" Woodrow said.

"Caroline thinks that goes over big," Taffy told him.

Woodrow leaned forward. "I never tried that myself."

Then Erica looked up and saw the group of us staring. She slapped George on the shoulder and he immediately put both of his feet flat on the ground and shrugged. They each picked up a shovel and walked away.

Woodrow shook his head. "I'll be damned." He walked over and poured himself another cup of coffee.

"If they fall in love and get married, you'll have to give us the family discount," I said.

"One conversation and you're marrying them off?" Taffy said.

"A person gets on a roll," Woodrow said.

Actually, George's love life was the furthest thing from my mind, but it was a comfort to know that if anything happened, Woodrow would be the one picking up the tab for the wedding.

As for the issue of that other wedding, I am ashamed to say that we had done absolutely nothing but worry ourselves sick over the whole thing. Every day Tom and I decided to call the Bennetts and explain our limitations to them, and every day we managed an admirable stall. A family's limitations seemed an especially private matter, and I wasn't any too eager to lay mine bare in front of people I didn't know. Instead I found myself trying to navigate the tricky extra bonus stamps on the Publisher's Clearing House Sweepstakes entry form.

"This isn't the answer," Tom said, picking up a series of color-coded coupons that had to be matched to a set of numbers that could only be found by reading ten pages of microprint. It would have been easier to file a hospital claim with our health insurance.

"What is the answer?"

"We call them."

"You know where the phone is," I said, going back to my forms.

Tom looked at the phone. It sat quietly on the kitchen table, goading us. "Maybe we should meet with the accountant first. That way we would know what we could offer to pay, realistically."

That seemed like a very reasonable plan to me. Tom was more than happy to call the accountant. An appointment was made and the stall was comfortably extended.

Kay, on the other hand, seemed a bundle of purpose and direction. She came by almost every night with a stack of books and planners and articles. She would spread her papers out across the dining-room table and study them so intently that it was almost like she was back in law school. Tom would wander in, but as soon as he saw that Kay wasn't working on a case, he would change directions and steer off toward the den. "There's a program on about the Galápagos," he'd say, trying to make it sound as if that was the reason he'd come in in the first place. "Does anybody else want to watch?"

Kay always smiled and shook her head. A minute later the television came on and we heard the sound of blue-footed boobies splashing into the warm sea.

"I can't believe how much there is to think about," Kay said. She tossed her pen down onto a copy of Martha Stewart's *Weddings* and rubbed her eyes. "I have my first meeting with Mrs. Carlson, the wedding planner, tomorrow and I'm supposed to come in with some ideas, but I don't even know where to start." She twisted her engagement ring around on her finger, the eternal flame. "You and Dad were so lucky to be able to just elope."

Was this the opening I had been dreaming of? Was she subtly asking my permission? "Everyone is allowed to elope," I said cautiously. "It's a noble tradition."

Kay rolled her eyes as if I was suggesting she buy a bag of silk worms and start spinning the thread for her dress. My plan was too fraught with difficulties to even consider. "I could never do that to people."

"Do what? Do it to whom?"

"Everyone would be so disappointed. Remember how disappointed Grandma was?"

I waved my hand. "You're only remembering half of the story. Ultimately she was very glad."

"Glad about what?" Taffy said, walking into the dining room and picking up a copy of *Bridal Guide*.

"Mom and Dad eloping," Kay said.

Taffy's face went ashen. She folded slowly into a chair. "Tell me you're not thinking about eloping. That was the worst thing that ever happened in our family when I was growing up."

"Oh, for God's sake, Taffy. You were eigh-

159

teen when I got married. What did you care?"

"I was sixteen and I wanted to be your maid of honor. I thought you eloped just because you didn't want me to be in your wedding."

I wondered if such a level of solipsism was possible, but I remembered my sister at eighteen and thought I would save myself the trouble of asking. "I wasn't the maid of honor at your wedding," I said. That was a prize that went to a plump girl with dark eyes named Lydia something or other who had been Taffy's best friend for that particular six-month period.

"Well, I certainly wasn't going to ask you after you didn't even invite me to your wedding."

"We didn't *have* a wedding."

Taffy put her hand over Kay's and squeezed. "This is why people should never elope," she said.

Kay gave me an insider's smile and shook her head as if to say, I never even thought about it in the first place, then she reached into her briefcase and pulled out a book of fabric samples. "If we can go back to the issue at hand for a minute, Mrs. Bennett says I really need to start thinking about choosing my colors."

Taffy picked up the fabric and got serious. If she decided not to teach tap at the studio, then maybe we could give her Mrs. Carlson's job and save some money, except that the idea of having Taffy around for that long was a little overwhelming.

I kept myself on a slow boil for the rest of the evening while I nodded my head in all the right places and agreed with every dress Kay pointed to in the magazines. At half past nine the doorbell rang. Kay shot out of her chair like a jackrabbit, clutching at her watch. "What time is it?"

"Expecting somebody?"

She started madly shoving her books and magazines back into her briefcase. There was a flutter of photographs, white dresses and satin shoes flipping between wedding cakes and sunny shots of Tahiti. "I'll get the door!"

But Kay wasn't having much luck with the door these days.

"Jack Carroll." We heard from the dining room.

"I remember you, Jack," Taffy said. "I remember all of Kay's friends."

Kay hoisted up her briefcase under one arm and suddenly Jack was there to take it from her. He had shaken off whatever grimness had weighed on him before and had reverted to his easy, charming self. "You were going to meet me," she said.

"Half an hour ago I was going to meet you," Jack said. I believe he had on exactly the same outfit he had worn the last time we saw him: the suit, the shirt, the tie — everything about Jack was wrinkled and familiar.

"Well, we should get going. Jack was going to go over a case with me. We should get to work." She patted her briefcase as if it were full of legal briefs.

"I thought you said you were at the D.A.'s office," Taffy said.

"Cross-pollination," Jack says. "It keeps us healthy."

"You should keep your voice down," I said to Kay. "Your father's in the other room."

Kay nodded and looked at the door. Jack checked out the room like someone who was hoping to find a plate of food. "Are you having a good visit?" he asked Taffy.

"A great visit," Kay said, and took the sleeve of his jacket firmly in one hand. "Let's go."

Jack picked up a rogue copy of *Bride's* and headed toward the door. "Good to see you both again," he said.

Taffy and I waved and said our good nights. Mercifully, Tom missed the whole party.

"That one worries me a little," Taffy said.

She was right. Kay making plans with Jack was more than a little suspicious at this point, but in my book it was nowhere near as serious as what Taffy had done. "She might have eloped," I said. "I could have talked her into it."

"Impossible," Taffy said. "Any woman who's bought that many bridal magazines has no intentions of eloping."

"She's the one who brought it up!"

Taffy shook her head. "And I always thought you were a better mother than I was. Don't you get it? It was all a test. She wants to know if you're really happy about this. You have to tell her that this wedding is important to you."

"It's only important to me insofar as it's going to destroy me."

"Look, Minnie, Kay is going to marry a Bennett, and it's going to be the biggest send-off since poor, unfortunate Diana landed the prince. Do you think she's going to cash that in for a trip to the courthouse where she works? You can't deal with this wedding by trying to stop it."

"I'm not trying to stop it," I said. "I just want her to know she has options."

"Don't kid yourself."

I folded my arms on the dining-room table and made a cradle for my head. "Did you really care that I eloped?"

Taffy sat down next to me and for a split second she put her hand on my shoulder. "For about five minutes. You know how I hate to miss a party."

163

chapter ten

We laid it all out for Annette, our accountant. We told her the truth. Usually when we
came in to tell her the truth about something, she wrote down numbers or tapped
things out on her calculator. She would have
all of our files spread out across her desk
and would sift through them while we ex-
plained things. But this time she just listened.
She folded her hands on the desk, leaned
forward, and let us talk. We didn't have to
give her the history. Annette had been doing
our taxes and badgering us to save for our
retirement since long before we could ever
have imagined we would one day retire. She
had been my student in ballet when she was
in junior high, though she didn't go all the
way with it. Annette's heart had always been
in numbers. She had known Kay all her life,
and while she didn't know Trey Bennett, she,
like every other citizen of Raleigh, knew just
about everything about him. Annette was
probably forty-five. She wasn't inclined toward exercise and she smoked. I knew her
well enough to nag her about it from time to

time. After all, she was familiar with every detail of my checking account. She had seen me through my most private moments of being overdrawn. It was very important to me to think that Annette was always going to be there.

Tom was nervous. Thinking about money always made him nervous, and thinking about the wedding made him a wreck. There was a light sheen of perspiration on his forehead and he was talking very fast. "We're guessing at the money in the first place. We've called some people, people whose children had big weddings, blowouts, and then we doubled it. If they're talking nine hundred guests —"

"It could be a thousand," I interjected. We might as well get it all out on the table.

Tom swallowed. That particular number was chilling. "Could be. A thousand. So we're guessing the total, and this is with the flowers and the band, I'm assuming a very fancy sit-down dinner for everyone, maybe seven hundred fifty thousand dollars? That's what people are telling us. I can't imagine that myself."

"My sister says it could go as high as a million."

"Her sister is from Atlanta," Tom said, as if the exchange rates were different in Atlanta and you just had to figure everything there was going to be 25 percent more expensive.

"I'm not asking for us to come up with five hundred thousand dollars. But the way I see it, we have to do something. We can't ask to do nothing. To not contribute. That wouldn't be right. Would that be right?" He turned to me and I shrugged.

"What's your best-case scenario?" Annette asked.

"Best case?" Tom mulled this one over. "Excluding elopement, excluding her suddenly falling in love with a poor guy who wants a reception in the church basement, excluding the chance that they decide to invite blood relatives only, I guess the best case is that the thing costs seven hundred fifty thousand dollars and we find a way to come up with half. So, best case, you help us find three hundred seventy-five thousand dollars."

Annette looked at Tom and looked at me. I thought she was going to say something, but when she opened her mouth, an enormous laugh escaped. She looked as surprised by it as we were, but she couldn't stop laughing. She put her hand over her mouth. "I'm sorry," she said. "I'm sorry." She closed her eyes and shook her head, but she was still laughing, her chest was convulsing. She couldn't pull it together. Annette excused herself, went out into the hallway, and closed her door. Tom and I sat in our matching chairs on the other side of the desk and looked at each other. We could still hear

Annette in the hall. Everything would be quiet for a second and then she would have another flare-up. It was as if she were trying to stamp down a bunch of small fires.

"Well, I guess we have a better idea of where we stand now," Tom said.

Annette came back holding several Kleenex and sat down at her desk. "Wow, *that* was unprofessional. I mean, if it had to happen, I'm glad it happened in front of the two of you, but still." She shook her head. "I mean, whew. It just came out of nowhere."

"Has it been happening a lot?" I asked.

"Well, I have the impulse all the time. People come in here and they say the most insane things — 'I'm just going to ask the IRS if I can take this year off,' that kind of craziness. I used to feel really concerned for them, but now it all just seems hysterical to me. I don't know. Maybe it's hormonal."

"So what you're telling us through your hysteria is that we aren't going to be able to get three hundred seventy-five thousand from the bank," Tom said.

"I'm sure it's there," Annette said. "But you'll have to go in with a ski mask and a gun to get it out, and that's not what I ever recommend to my clients, especially my favorite clients." Another little chortle escaped her but she got right on top of it.

"Realistically, then," I said.

"Realistically." She pulled over her little

adding machine and a sheet of numbers. Annette's fingers could really fly, and I thought that if she had learned how to do that with her feet in junior high, she would have been a star on Broadway. I liked the steady tap and then the mechanical expulsion of the paper. It always felt so promising, like the lottery numbers were coming down the chute. "Now, this is a ballpark, this is rounded. For something more exact I'm going to need a little time."

"Just tell us," Tom said.

"Ten thousand dollars."

We looked at her. Ten thousand dollars? "That would cover the rice they throw as the couple is getting into the car." Assuming they planned on using some sort of pearl-grain rice hand-grown by Tibetan monks.

"That's all we've got?" Tom said.

"Oh, no," Annette said. "You don't even have that. You had the fund for the Florida room and the fund for the retirement trip to Italy, but we're assuming that both of those things are going into the foundation of your house at the moment. Then you're going to need to pay off the addition, unless you decide to scrap it, which may cost you almost as much as finishing it at this point. You've got a little money for your share of George's law school and you're not throwing that away on a wedding. So the ten thousand is going to be another home equity loan. The only other place it could come from would be your retirement account, and that's not happening."

"But it could," Tom said.

"No, it could not," Annette said. She leaned back in her chair and looked at us with a great deal of compassion. She had two girls who were teenagers now. She knew that sooner or later this would be happening to her, too. "Listen, the rich aren't like you and me. They forget things, like the fact that everybody else isn't rich. Sometimes they even forget that they have an enormous amount of money themselves. So they asked you to pay for half of this thing and you can't. Just own up to it. I know it's humiliating, but it's a fact. The numbers don't lie. You can't pay for the kind of wedding they're talking about. What you have to remember is that ten thousand dollars is a lot of money, and there are a whole lot of people out there who would fall over dead from a heart attack if you said you could spend ten thousand on your daughter's wedding. You've got to keep it in perspective."

She gave us each a peppermint from the bowl she kept on the desk and she sent us on our way.

When we left we were broken, defeated. We sat in the parking lot behind her office in the cold car, but Tom didn't make a move to turn it on.

"If I had stayed corporate . . ." Tom started.

He did this every now and then. I will admit that a couple of times over the years I had done it myself but always silently. It was the kind of game that was best not to play. "You would be a full partner, your name on the stationery. You would be making a fortune and you would be miserable, so none of it would be worthwhile." I reached out and squeezed his hand. "You can't call your whole life into question just because we can't pay for Kay to have a wedding with nine hundred people she doesn't even know. Those are not the standards by which we're going to judge ourselves. I refuse to."

Tom looked at me. His eyes were tired behind his glasses and his skin was pale. When did we get to be so old? "I could have done everything another way. There was a fork in the road and I went left. For a long time I thought I was doing the right thing, but now I'm not so sure."

"You did the right thing, and anyway, you can't go back to that fork. It isn't an option to change everything now."

"I wanted to be in the courtroom. I wanted to defend people. What was the point of being a lawyer if you couldn't defend people? It was the only thing that made sense to me."

"So you did the right thing."

Tom's voice was worn out, defeated. He was looking back on all the nights he'd slept on the couch in his office getting ready to go to trial, all the peanut-butter crackers he'd eaten from the vending machine. "But they weren't the people I thought they'd be. I mean, some of them were, a few of them, but there were a lot of bad people over the years, people who didn't care about anything, people who were guilty. I feel like I gave up making a good life for my family so I could defend people who were guilty."

"Listen, you've got to stop this. This is a wedding. This is about cages of white doves and a five-thousand-dollar cake and a whole bunch of valet parkers who are all dressed alike. You're talking about regretting a whole life devoted to the most fundamentally important things you believe in. You can't regret that just because we can't pay for this wedding."

Tom was quiet for a while. Even when one of us was really worked up about something, we still managed to listen to the other one. I liked to think it was the thing that had made this marriage possible. "I can regret it for a little while," he said mildly.

I leaned across the space between our seats and put my head on his shoulder. Oh, how I longed for the days of bench seats in cars. "Okay," I said. "I won't stop you."

★ ★ ★

I dropped Tom off at the office and went home to get ready for class. Maybe now we understood absolutely that we couldn't pay for half of the wedding, but we were no closer to understanding how we were going to break the news to the Bennetts or, worse yet, to Kay. As I was walking in the house, I had the sinking feeling that nothing had really changed at all, except that Tom had been given the opportunity to beat himself up over not making more money. When I came into the kitchen, Taffy was talking on the phone and Stamp was standing on the kitchen table licking a clean butter dish, which I believe had had a half stick of butter on it when I left the house this morning.

"Stamp!" I said. "You get down from there right now!"

Stamp looked up at me, wagged his missing tail, and went back to work on the dish. Taffy gave me a hard stare and put her hand over the receiver. "I'm on the phone," she said.

"Well, the dog certainly seems to understand that." I went to pick Stamp up, but he looked at me and growled. I was furious. The audacity of that dog, after I had given him a roof over his head, and the time of my busy contractor for what seemed to be his unsuccessful lessons, and the calf of my husband, who had enough to worry about without

172

being bitten by a dog, a dog who was never invited to visit in the first place!

"So why did you decide that you had to call him now, anyway?" Taffy said into the phone.

"Don't you *dare* growl at me!" I picked him up and dropped him unceremoniously onto the floor, at which point he immediately hopped back up on a chair on his way to the table. I lifted my hand. *"Ah!"* I said loudly, mimicking Woodrow. Stamp stopped and thought about it for a minute. He knew the butter was gone as well as I did. He got off the chair, went under the table, and lay down.

"Would you *stop* talking to the dog!" Taffy shouted.

I looked at my sister, whose face, I had failed to notice before, was red, her eyes watery. She turned away from me and bent over the receiver. "It was every bit as much my right to call him as it was yours. . . . Well then, I'm just the one who thought of it first."

I went over and stood beside her. I put my hand on her shoulder, but she shook it off. "So you'll find somebody else. You seem so good at finding somebody else. When you do, have him call Buddy Lewis. . . . No, I'm not going to talk about this. . . . You can't have your way every time, Neddy. That's not the way it works. You don't get to have everything just because you want it. . . . Yes. Yes, I understand. All right, then." Taffy hung up the phone. She looked at me. She seemed almost frantic.

"What happened?" I said quietly.

"Goddamn Neddy. He called Buddy Lewis. He finally got around to calling the divorce lawyer, and when he found out that Buddy was representing me, he just went ballistic. He said I've got to give him back Buddy Lewis. Is that the most insane thing you've ever heard?"

"Why do you have to give him back?"

"Neddy says they're friends. He says they play golf together and Buddy doesn't want to represent me. He says I never even would have thought about calling Buddy Lewis if it wasn't for him, that I wouldn't even have known his name, which isn't true because all of my friends who got divorced used Buddy Lewis. Anybody who's ever been unhappy in their marriage and lives in Atlanta knows who Buddy Lewis is."

"So you told him no?"

Taffy rested her forehead against her hands and she cried and cried. It was the grief of a child who cried from a fever, a girl who cried out of the frustration of her age, a young woman who had lost her young husband to war. Taffy cried and Stamp came from under the table and jumped up on her lap. Taffy held him to her face and cried into his neck while I stroked her hair. "He's going to divorce me," she said. "He's really going to divorce me."

There was nobody else at home. George was in school and Woodrow and his group were off somewhere adding on a master bedroom that they were already late in starting because they'd spent too much time over here. We were all alone, me and Taffy and Stamp. I stroked my sister's hair. Every now and then Stamp would look up at me and lick my wrist.

Taffy pulled it together but it took a while. I made us some coffee and we sat and drank it.

"I guess I thought he wouldn't go through with it," Taffy said. "The way he's been calling all the time and he never mentioned anything. I guess I'd let myself think that I was just on vacation, that we were working things out and that I would go home and, I don't know, that we'd forget about it."

"That would be a lot to forget," I said.

Taffy nodded. "But I could have." She took each of Stamp's ears between her fingers and rubbed the thin leather of skin. The light shone through them when she held them up and turned them pink. "About that job . . ."

"You can have a job."

"I should do that. Minnie, I know you must hate me. I'm sorry that I'm staying for so long."

"I don't hate you at all. You can stay for as long as you want."

"It might be a while. At least this way I can be a little helpful. I think Woodrow was right. I'm going to go crazy if I just sit around here all day and do nothing."

"Maybe you can tap your way through this," I said, trying to be a little lighthearted. "That's the way I've gotten through everything awful in my life."

Taffy looked up and gave me a sad half-smile. "What's ever been so awful in your life?"

I had to think about it. There had been a miscarriage between Charlie and Kay. There had been the time when things were bad with Tom. There had been worries over money, always there had been worries over money, but I could see that compared to Taffy, coming out of a marriage that hadn't been so good to begin with, my life had been blessed. I wasn't an especially religious person, but that was the only word I could come up with. She had been beautiful and rich and I had been blessed. "Nothing," I said. "Nothing has been so awful."

She took a drink of her coffee and nodded like she had won the argument. "So, how did things go at the accountant's?"

"Well, maybe I should change my answer. The trip to the accountant's was pretty awful." I looked at my watch. Somehow we had fallen into the black hole of time. "I need to get going. I have a tap class at three."

"I'll take it."

"Give yourself a break," I said. "You've had a horrible day."

"So have you. I want to get to work."

"So get to work tomorrow."

Taffy shook her head. "Let's go ahead and settle this thing once and for all. I've been looking over the schedule. I want the Intro to Tap, Beginning Tap, and Beginning Ballet."

"You took ballet, too?"

"Ten years."

"If your marriage hadn't broken up, I never would have known a thing about you."

"I'm going to take a shower. You don't have to come to the school with me. I'm going to be fine. Stay home and balance your checkbook, or why don't you take the quiet time to call Lila Bennett? Tell her that you've been thinking it over, and not only are you not going to pay for the wedding, you think they should pay you for the right to have Kay in the family."

"How much?"

Taffy thought about it. For a minute she got the same look on her face as Annette had, as if she were running up a column of numbers in her head. "Half a million."

"For Kay?"

"Oh, she's worth it. I think you could get even more than that."

Taffy left for school and a little after that George called and said that he was going to be in his study group until midnight. He said that he hadn't been called on yet in his Torts class and he was having a dark premonition that tomorrow was his day. I took Stamp for a walk and then I came home and sat down in front of the phone. It was a harmless little chunk of plastic and wires. I used it almost every day. I would pick it up now and call Lila Bennett. I wouldn't talk it over with Tom first. That would be my gift to him. He would come home and I would say, Guess what I did today?

My hands were sweating. I got up and poured myself a glass of wine. I sat down again to call, but Stamp was looking at me and I thought it didn't really seem fair that I was getting a treat and he wasn't. I had some liverwurst in the refrigerator.

"Liverwurst?" I said.

The dog shot straight up in the air. Suddenly the floor was a trampoline. Every time he hit it, he sprung back higher. "Liverwurst?" I said. "Liverwurst?"

It was a word he knew. A word that meant more to him than *sit* or *come* or *stay*. He was jumping as high as the table, and I said the word over and over while I rifled through the refrigerator for the plastic Baggie of braun-schweiger. I was laughing hysterically. I loathed Stamp, but sometimes even I had to admit that there had never been a more entertaining dog. I took a big gulp of wine and sang out our new favorite word. "Li-ver-wurst, liverwurst, liverwurst, li-ver-wurst!" I was laughing and Stamp was barking hysterically and then the phone rang.

"Hell-o-o," I said to the tune of "Liver-wurst."

"Caroline?" the voice said.

"Speaking." Stamp could do a back flip in the air if Woodrow set his mind to teach him. I was sure of it.

"It's Lila Bennett."

At that moment the nearly full tube of liverwurst slipped from my fingers. Stamp caught it in midair and was gone, gone, gone.

"Hello," I said, wishing there was a cordless phone in the kitchen so I could run after the dog before he killed himself, wishing I had never answered the phone in the first place, wishing I were dead.

"How wonderful that I caught you in. I'm sitting here with Mrs. Carlson. The wedding planner? Did Kay tell you? We had such a productive meeting. We have several colors to go with, depending on the time of year. Caroline, I have got to be able to count on you for help. We need to get a date set and it simply cannot be six months from now. What's that? Hold the line for one minute, will you?"

"Yes, of course." I clamped my hand over the receiver and called for the dog, but I may as well have been calling for Paul Newman to show up and refill my glass. I polished off the wine.

"Mrs. Carlson was just agreeing with me. With these kinds of numbers, it isn't going to be possible to do this in less than a year. Not possible."

"I understand." The cord was long enough to get me back to the refrigerator.

"Brilliant! Then we're all on the same page. I'll need you to meet with me and Mrs. Carlson very soon."

"I have something I need to talk to you about," I said weakly. I pulled out the cork with one hand.

"Is next week all right? We can talk about everything. Don't think these colors are set in stone. Anything Kay shows you is just a suggestion. We want your input on this one hundred percent."

"About the wedding . . ."

"Exactly. I don't have my book in front of me. My secretary can call you. Is that all right? I don't want to give you a date I can't keep."

"Of course," I said.

"Perfect," she said. "Thank you. Tell me,

don't you think this is all a dream?"

When I found Stamp it was already too late. The bedroom looked like a crime scene. A dog can eat his own weight in liverwurst in under a minute. He was stretched out on Tom's pillow, bits of heavy processed meat still clinging to the hairs of his muzzle. The used package lay spent about six inches from his back paw. It was only plastic. It didn't stand a chance. When I sat down on the bed, he never looked up. In one afternoon the dog had consumed half a stick of butter and probably eight ounces of liverwurst. I considered calling the vet to see if I needed to have his stomach pumped, but probably he just needed to sleep it off. The hairless skin of his belly seemed to strain as he breathed. I wondered if it ever happened that dogs simply exploded.

I reached over and picked up the phone and dialed Tom's office. "I'm in bed with Stamp," I said.

"I should have known it would turn out like this. What is the dog wearing?"

"Liverwurst." At the mention of the word, Stamp opened one eye and did a slow, meaningful thump with his tail stub.

"Sounds sexy," Tom said.

"You want to hear something even sexier than that?"

"I'm listening."

"I'm home alone." It was the first time it

had happened since the night Kay called to tell us she was getting married.

"How do you define alone?"

"No other higher mammals in the house. Woodrow hasn't come over at all today, George has a study group, and Taffy is teaching until seven. It's just me and Stamp."

"Put the dog outside," Tom said. "I'll be right there."

Tom and I had been married for forty-two years. We had four children. I'm not saying we had sex all the time. Certainly weeks had gone by before. Over the course of so many years there had been times that months had gone by. But when we couldn't make love, when the house was too full and we were too overwhelmed by the world around us, we were both keenly aware of the lack of opportunity. We leaned into each other while brushing our teeth in the morning, we touched feet while drinking coffee. Sometimes we wanted the sex, but other times we just wanted the privacy that sex represented. We wanted to feel profoundly together and alone in a way that comes most easily when two people are in bed. I picked Stamp up, carried his bloated body into Taffy's room, and closed the door. Usually he was a dog who wanted to be with people, but I think, given the circumstances, he could have cared less. I took a two-minute shower to get the smell of terrier and liverwurst off of me and then I wrapped myself up in Tom's bathrobe. I had just dried my feet when I heard his car pull up in the driveway, and I was down the hall as he opened the door. We stood there and kissed for a long time, a fulfillment of the promises made in all the little kisses we had exchanged over the last couple of weeks, then we went back to the bedroom and locked the door. We were used to locking the door. It never hurt to be safe.

The sun was just going down and we were lying there reveling in the silence of our house. "It was very nice of you to call," Tom said.

"I'm glad you were free." I wanted to go to sleep. It was an impossible time of day to take a nap and Taffy would be home from class soon. If you fall asleep once it's dark, you really are done for. "You want to hear something really funny?"

"Tell me something funny." Tom pulled me closer.

"I almost called Lila Bennett today to tell her we couldn't pay for the wedding. I was going to do it as a surprise."

"That's incredibly sweet." He gave me a lazy kiss on the part of my hair. "What stopped you?"

"She called me first. I was sitting right there, my hand was practically on the phone."

"I hate it when that happens."

"She wants to go over the colors next week with Mrs. Carlson, the wedding planner. She wants me to know she cares about my input on the colors."

"Well, she won't care once she finds out you're broke. She'll plan a lime-green wedding for our daughter and there won't be anything you can do to stop her."

Suddenly there was a flash of headlights through the bedroom window and Tom and I both sat bolt upright in bed.

"Get dressed," Tom said, hopping into his pants.

I rolled over and grabbed for my underwear. "Can you see who it is?"

Tom glanced out of the window, somehow managing to zip up his pants and pull on his shirt in one fluid motion. "It's too dark."

I found a sweater on the floor and some loose jazz pants. We heard the front door swing open. This was not doorbell company.

"Mom? Dad?"

Tom raked his hand deftly through his hair and hit the hallway. "Hey there, we're back here."

"What are you guys doing back there? The house is so dark, I didn't think anyone was home."

"Your mother found another crack in the ceiling," I heard him say. The secret to a good lie was to tell them something they would believe.

I had a minute now and I ran a brush through my hair and pinned it back up again. When I came into the kitchen, Kay was already pulling out a stack of papers from her bag. "Hi, honey."

"Where's Taffy?"

"She's teaching a tap class."

"Taffy can dance?"

"Turns out she's great."

Kay looked around the kitchen hopefully. "Have you guys eaten already?"

"I'll call for pizza," Tom said.

"Perfect, count me in. Just tell them to hold the olives. I hate olives."

"I know you hate olives," Tom said, going to look up the number. "Do you think I just got here?"

Kay put a cluster of fabric swatches and paint cards out on the table. Most of them were in the family of either ashy blue or pale moss green. Impeccably tasteful. "Mrs. Bennett wanted me to show you the colors. She's afraid you're going to feel excluded. And Dad, I want to go over this deposition I have for tomorrow. I don't think the arrest looks clean at all."

chapter eleven

A whole week had gone by and Neddy hadn't called. I had thought that all of his previous irritating phone calls for how to get the garage door opener to work (change the batteries) or how he could get his groceries delivered to the house (Taffy called their housekeeper and made arrangements for her to do the shopping) would have been depressing for Taffy, but the silence proved to be infinitely worse. Around seven o'clock, the time the phone used to ring, she would sit in the kitchen drinking a glass of wine and dabbing her eyes on her sleeve while she pretended to look at a magazine. Every night without a call seemed to drive the reality of her new life closer to home.

"I called him about sending me my mail and he didn't even pick up the phone," Taffy said. "Maybe I should just give in."

"Give in on what?" Tom asked.

"I should give him my divorce lawyer. That's why he's giving me the cold shoulder. He's sulking. When he sulks long enough, I always give him his own way."

"Why does he want your divorce lawyer?"

"Because whoever gets Buddy Lewis always winds up winning in the end."

Tom squatted down in front of Taffy and put his hands on her knees. "Listen to me, as a brother-in-law and a lawyer: You want to win. Good for you for calling this guy first."

"How do I know why he isn't calling? Maybe it has nothing to do with Buddy. Neddy could be lying dead on the floor, and who would know it?"

"Taffy, he isn't dead," I said.

"Let me dream," she said, and slammed her magazine closed.

On a brighter note, she was a huge hit at the dance studio, so much so that I might have felt a little threatened by it if I didn't feel so sorry for her. Taffy was a tougher teacher than I was. She did not tolerate whispering or horsing around of any fashion. Nor did she tolerate sloppy stepping. If someone didn't know the steps, there was no shame in that, she would say, but we weren't here to simply fake it and move on to the next routine. Taffy, who hadn't had a real job since she gave tennis lessons at the country club the summer before she got married, liked professionalism. She liked order. While I thought her standards might be a bit too rigorous for little girls, they all seemed to love it. Whenever I taught one of Taffy's classes, I noticed that we started exactly on time, forgoing the normal ten minutes of questions and giggling, the rows at the barre were straighter, and everyone kept her shoulders back. In short, Taffy had brought some good old Marine sensibility to McSwan's, although I can't imagine where she had picked it up to begin with.

"That's the way I am with Neddy," she said. "I guess it just came to me over the years. He's such a big slob, you know, a great big self-indulgent kid. If I didn't take a hard line with Neddy, he'd sit home and eat M&M's all day. He used to call me the General, but he liked it. He'd say, 'General, if it weren't for you, I wouldn't be able to find my toes.' I never knew if that meant he'd forget where he'd put them or he'd just get too fat to see them." Taffy looked at her wedding ring. She twisted it around a couple of times on her finger. She had an engagement ring that we all thought was the biggest thing we'd ever seen until we saw Kay's. "Isn't that odd, the way I said he liked me bossing him around? Maybe he didn't like it at all. Maybe that's why he left me."

It was a combination of unbearable darkness and unbearable light around the Mc-Swain house, and I had no idea which one I found more perplexing: Taffy's heartbreak over the loss of Neddy and his phone calls or Kay's constant euphoria in trying to draw up a list of bridesmaids. The emotional barometer of our house shot up and down at any given hour. The two people who seemed to deal with it best were Kay and Taffy, who were each endlessly considerate of the other's feelings.

"I think that calla lilies would be perfect for the bridesmaids' bouquets," Taffy would say.

"Have you talked to Neddy anymore?" Kay would ask.

It was in this sea of uncertainty that I decided to throw Taffy a surprise party for what she claimed to be her fifty-eighth and I knew to be her sixtieth birthday. There would be no people hiding in the closets with sparklers, no flashing a camera the minute the lights went on. It would just be a nicer-than-usual dinner at which everyone was present. I didn't want to tell Taffy about it only because I knew she was in no mood to celebrate anything, much less herself, but I wanted to at least take a stab at cheering her up.

Four nights later I asked Taffy to teach both the afternoon and the evening classes, and I made a rack of lamb with rosemary, new potatoes and asparagus with blueberries. I felt as though I hadn't cooked in years, and I took some satisfaction in the salad and the smooth icing on the lemon cake. I'd bought Taffy a very fancy pair of black tap shoes with a two-inch heel and wrapped them up in a box with gold ribbon. I always tapped in flats, but I knew Taffy would like the heel. The house was as clean as the house could get under the present circumstances, and I'd cleared all of Kay's wedding paraphernalia off the dining-room table and put out some African daisies I'd bought at the grocery store for a center-piece. I lit the candles and took a long look at the picture: It was as close to *Martha Stewart Living* as I was ever going to get. Taffy was the first to arrive and she seemed happy and grateful, either that I had remembered her birthday or that she now had the time to grab a quick shower and change out of her dance clothes before the guests arrived.

The guest list in its original form was what anyone would have suspected: Tom and me, Trey and Kay, George, Woodrow, and Taffy. I invited Woodrow because he was one of the only people in town who Taffy knew, and besides, I had an ulterior motive: He hadn't been over all week and I thought by inviting him to the party he would come to realize how much he missed us. Then, in a move of superior good manners, I called Trey and invited him myself. Sure, we weren't a fancy bunch, but if he was going to be a member of the family, he might as well start coming to the birthday parties now.

Taffy's Surprise Party: Surprises listed in ascending order.

SURPRISE #1: Woodrow arrives in a sport coat and blue bow tie.

A small point but one definitely worth mentioning. Woodrow had been at my house on and off for three months, and I had never seen him wearing anything but a thermal underwear top and a pair of paint-splattered overalls. The colors changed but the look was always the same. He usually had some drywall in his hair by the end of the day and, without realizing it, that was how I had come to think of him, as a man with drywall in his hair. But when the doorbell rang, there stood Woodrow wearing a sport coat and a blue bow tie, looking not at all like the man who spent so much time crawling around under my house. Not enough men wear bow ties, if you ask me. Tom always said the jury would never take him seriously in one. But I can tell you they certainly would have taken Woodrow seriously. He came with a very nice bottle of French white wine and a wrapped box for Taffy.

SURPRISE #2: Another member of the Woodrow family arrives.

"Mom," George said as he walked in the back door. "I invited Erica to come to dinner tonight. I hope that's okay."

I turned around and there stood the radiant Erica with her high heels and bare legs and her hair pulled back into the same tight bun she wore to do construction work. She

191

held herself like a young woman who had danced ballet every day of her life. There is nothing more enticing than good posture. I was extremely glad to see her and calculated another place at the table. "Of course it's okay. Erica, I'm delighted that you're here." As I kissed her cheek, I tried to remember the last time I'd seen George. It had been days. Many days. With his study sessions and peculiar student hours, I often didn't see him for long stretches of time, but now there was a light going on in my head.

"You told me your mother invited me to dinner," Erica said to George.

"I had every intention of inviting you," I said.

"Don't cover for him," Erica said kindly. I could tell she wanted to kick George in the shins.

"Erica?" Woodrow said, walking into the kitchen to fix himself a drink.

"Daddy?"

"Woodrow's here!" George said. "That's terrific! Erica, your dad's here."

"I can see my dad's here." Erica pulled her blue shawl higher up on her shoulders.

"It's my sister's birthday," I said, trying to explain it to Erica, trying to make her feel as though she hadn't been ambushed. "You remember my sister, Taffy?"

"It's a *birthday* party?" Erica said. She closed her eyes.

SURPRISE #3: Kay has two dates.

Enter my beautiful girl, already on the course of bridal radiance. There was a time not so long ago that Kay would have come over wearing jeans and a Duke Law sweatshirt, with a licorice whip hanging out of her mouth. But those days were gone. Always she wears lipstick now, always her blunt cut looks freshly shorn, as if she stopped by the hairdresser's on her way to work every morning. I wondered if she'd started having facials or if it was just the glow that came with making lists of all the things you wanted.

"Where's Trey?" I said.

Kay shrugged sweetly and whispered in my ear, "I told Jack he could come. He's been driving me crazy lately. We're kind of working through this whole separation thing. He says he wants to still be able to spend time with my family."

"Hey, Mrs. McSwain!" Jack swung into the room and kissed my cheek. I have already made note of his looks and there is no need to go over it again. This guy had one outfit or he had many outfits all crushed to look like the same outfit. He managed to keep an extremely consistent layer of stubble on his cheek. He managed to look like the sexy rogue in a beer ad.

"Jack, hello! Kay, sweetheart, I'm going to need you in the kitchen for one minute."

Off we went through the swinging kitchen

door, which was closed to give the dining room the dressier look it never achieves. I took her shoulders in my hands. "What in the hell are you doing with Jack?" I knew this was not the place I should be starting. We had a lot of ground to cover in a very short period of time.

"Jack is a friend of mine, you know that." Kay was using her lawyer tone on me and it did not work.

"We're meeting with wedding planners, we're talking about colors, we're spending every evening poring over dresses, and you're showing up at your aunt's birthday party with your old boyfriend?"

"He's a *friend*, Mother. There is nothing going on between Jack and me. You know I love Trey."

"That's great. Tell him that when he gets here for dinner."

Kay blinked and then she cocked her head to one side. It was a look Stamp sometimes gave me when he was trying to figure out what in the hell I was talking about. "Trey's not coming to dinner," she said calmly.

"I invited him. I called him."

Now her eyes were open wide. "How could you! How could you do that to me?"

"I was being polite. I thought surely you'd told him. I told you to invite him. I was just —"

Doorbell.

Kay grabbed me. "I'll get the door, you tell Jack."

There was no discussion this time. She was out of there as fast as a wire-haired fox terrier with a mouth full of liverwurst. I slipped through the door in one of its mad crashes back and forth, the wake of Kay's panic. "Jack? Could I see you in the kitchen for just one minute?"

Jack ambled in, a beer in his hand, Irish charm and Irish trouble written all over him. "Can I help with dinner?"

"Can you help with dinner," I said, thinking about it. "Yes, really, you can. There isn't a lot of time, so I'll get right to the point. Kay invited you to dinner and I invited Trey, so you're going to have to go out there and make yourself look very much like the friend of the family that you keep telling everybody you are."

Jack was taking it in. There was no great look of glee on his face. Then Taffy swung through the door with her empty glass.

"He's here again," she said to me, looking at Jack.

"There's been a little mix-up," he said sadly.

"I should say so. I was just talking to the future bridegroom in the living room."

"I should go," Jack said.

He was something, that one. I could see why Kay would have a hard time shaking him off. He looked so utterly defeated that I wanted to put my arms around him. He was charming when he was happy, but he was irresistible when he was sad.

"Don't do it," Taffy said. She was in a bright mood, wearing a set of gold silk hostess pajamas with a long strand of pearls that no one in their right mind would have packed for a visit to Raleigh, but she looked fantastic. In spite of all the things that had changed, she was still my little sister, a girl who loved parties and loved them best when they were for her. "We'll just say you're my date." She put her hand on his arm. "Taffy was always crazy about Kay's friend Jack. They hit it off so well together."

"He wouldn't dream of missing her birthday party," Jack said, gratefully putting his hand over hers.

"She wouldn't even have a party without him."

"You know I owe you for this," Jack said.

"Maybe we'll owe each other. It's still your responsibility to cheer me up."

And off they went to the party. I went into the cupboards and took out another place setting. If the doorbell didn't ring again, I could avoid putting another leaf in the table.

SURPRISE #4: The doorbell rings again.
Despite all the reconfiguration, everyone seemed to be having a very good time. Erica

196

was talking to Trey about the hospital where she was doing her student nursing, which happened to be a hospital his parents owned, and they both agreed it was an excellent facility. Taffy was talking to Woodrow about where he had been and how Stamp seemed to be having a relapse in his absence. George was rhapsodizing to Jack about the fabulousness that was Erica. Kay was talking to her father about a case, but mostly she was sneaking off glances at Trey and then Jack, and I thought maybe it was good for her to have them both in the same room, where she could do some serious competitive evaluations and make up her mind once and for all. I was serving my cheese puffs, which had turned out magnificently. Everyone was milling about and drinking and paying Taffy lavish compliments, which was what people really wanted for their birthday.

When the doorbell rang, I briefly had the thought, Who now? I was sure that there was no one left to come to the party. It was probably the Christian missionaries of my imagination, come to see if I was still interested in being saved.

When I opened the door, I knew what I should have gotten for Taffy for her birthday. I should have tracked down Holden and invited her to the party. The truth is, I'd never even considered it, and yet there she stood, with an armload of presents. She raised one finger to her lips and I stepped outside and shut the door behind me.

"Holden!" I wrapped my arms around my niece, knocking a couple of the gifts to the ground, but who cared? I was thrilled that she was there, and at the same time I realized she should have been there weeks ago.

"I wanted to surprise Mother," she said.

Had this woman come from any part of our family? Her hair was long and blond and stick straight. She was tall, and with her pale skin and red lipstick, her black T-shirt that looked like it cost three hundred dollars, I thought she should have been a movie star rather than wasting her time representing them. She had all of her mother's beauty, all of her mother's poise, but her look was glamorous whereas Taffy's was soft. There was a black Porsche 911 parked in front of the house.

"You drove?"

Holden looked behind her shoulder. "That? No, I rented it at the airport."

"You can rent a Porsche?"

"You can rent anything," she said, smiling. "How's Mom?"

I reached up and touched her hair. It was cool and heavy. "She's been awful and okay. She's going to be a million times better now that you're here."

"I should have come sooner. It's just been crazy. We had a lot of luck at Cannes and then there were so many deals to close. I thought I'd get away last week, and then yesterday I looked at my schedule and I just thought, Get on a plane."

"She's going to be so happy. We're having a party for her."

"A surprise party?"

"It's certainly turning into one." I picked up the presents and rearranged them in Holden's arms. The gold foil paper from the packages reflected the light onto her face and made her shine. Holden had such a genius for details. She'd probably picked the paper with that in mind.

We came inside and I closed the door behind us. "Who was it?" Tom said, walking into the entry hall. He broke out into a huge smile when he saw Holden there. Silently, he kissed her cheek and then stepped aside so she could be the first one in the room. She made a perfect entrance — the boxes, the pink from the cool night air still in her cheeks. The whole room turned and fell silent at the sight of her.

"Happy Birthday, Mother."

Tom leaned over and took the boxes away just as Taffy stepped into Holden's arms. A second later Stamp raced across the room, jumping up higher than he had for the liverwurst until Taffy and Holden were forced apart and Holden caught the dog in midair and held him. He was so ecstatic that he twisted and wrenched in her arms, as if he was trying to get even closer to her as she held him.

Jack the D.A. leaned over and whispered in my ear, his voice stunned as if from a sharp blow. "Who's the goddess?"

"That's my niece, Holden."

"Dear Lord," he said.

It had been good before, but now it was really a party. The champagne meant for toasts with the cake was broken out before dinner. Holden saw Kay's engagement ring and threw her arms around her neck. "You're getting married! That's brilliant. Look at this ring! My God, Elizabeth Taylor must be sweating out her status as having the best engagement ring." Holden looked at the group. "First she's a lawyer and now she's getting married. No wonder I never come home. I always feel like such an underachiever."

Everyone laughed as if she'd said something very funny. Holden put her hand on Jack's arm and squeezed. "Are you the lucky one?"

"I'm lucky," he said, never giving Kay a look. "I'm not that lucky."

"Then who are you?" she asked.

"Leftovers," Jack said. "Jack Carroll."

"I'm Trey Bennett." Trey held out his hand but Holden kissed him instead. "The groom! Then you're the lucky man. You have to promise to give her everything she wants.

This is my very favorite cousin. Forgive me, George. My favorite female cousin." She leaned her head against Kay's shoulder. "This man is gorgeous," she said, sotto voce, fully intending to be heard by everyone. Trey blushed in gratitude. Holden immediately lifted the glass Tom handed her. "To my beautiful, lucky cousin. I drink to your engagement. And to my wonderful mother on her birthday. I am so happy to be with you!"

"Hear! Hear!" called the crowd.

Woodrow watched the scene with appreciation. "The apple doesn't fall very far from the tree," he said to my sister.

There was a strange muffled bleating sound, as if someone had left a sheep in the coat closet. Holden shrugged with mock embarrassment. "I'm sorry." She slipped her hand inside her Tod's bag. "That's me." She took out a phone the size of two credit cards sewn together and she flipped it open. "Holden," she said. Her voice had the same clipped edge that her mother's had when teaching a tap class. "Did you get the fax? We have the papers until the twenty-third. That's right. Then get them signed." She flipped the phone shut without saying good-bye. "When does it all end?" she said.

"This is Erica Woodrow," George said, presenting her to Holden. "And this is her father, Woodrow."

Holden shook their hands and expressed

her real pleasure in meeting them. "George can dance," she said to Erica. "Do you know how hard it is to find a man who can dance?"

"I'm not much of a dancer myself," Erica admitted.

"It doesn't matter. He's like Fred Astaire. He can make anyone look good on a dance floor. Not that you need any help looking good."

Holden passed out compliments evenly and sincerely. We all felt amazed that someone so worldly seemed to enjoy our humble company. As she worked her way across the room, she managed to make every person there feel that he or she was the one she had most wanted to see.

"Isn't this all so divine?" she said.

It was all we could do to make ourselves sit down and eat the lamb before it was well-done. Taffy sat on one side of her daughter, and with the aid of some simple diversion tactics, Jack managed to swing into the chair on Holden's other side. I thought I detected a slight cloud of irritation cross Kay's face but, like the rest of the party, I was too entranced with Holden to care. Holden made no attempt to dominate the conversation, but people kept asking her questions. She rewarded them with stories about movie stars and the South of France. She shamelessly ratted out her clients for our entertainment, and Taffy basked in the glow of her extended light.

Holden let Stamp sit in her lap while she ate and Woodrow didn't say a word about it. "I begged them to use Stamp for the lead in *My Dog Skip*," she said. "In the book the dog is a fox terrier, not a Jack Russell. That other dog was all wrong for the part."

"So how did it fall through?" Woodrow asked.

Holden crushed the dog against her breast and every man in the room sighed. "Stamp had too many scruples. He wasn't willing to sleep with the right people."

"You never told me you had a cousin," Trey said to Kay.

"Doesn't everyone have cousins? You probably have hundreds of cousins you haven't told me about."

"She's my cousin, too, you know," George said. "Other boys used to have pictures of Heather Locklear in their lockers, but I always had one of Holden in mine."

"Isn't that slightly creepy?" Erica asked.

"It's creepy when you're thirty, but when you're thirteen it's pretty endearing."

Erica smiled and George took her hand and held it. It would take a lot more than a cousin to knock out Erica Woodrow's self-esteem.

Kay, on the other hand, had always walked the fine line between adoring her only girl cousin, like the rest of the world did, and being jealous of her. Holden cast a longer shadow than any girl in Atlanta.

The sheep in the closet let out another plaintive bleat. "Isn't this awful? At the dinner table." But even as she was saying it, she was reaching into her purse. "Holden." Her face melted into a smile. "Darling. No, of course I don't mind. Don't be silly, that's why I gave you the number."

No one could say a word. We couldn't even pretend to be whispering about something else. There was nothing to do but sit there and take in every word of the conversation.

"I saw the rushes and I thought they were gorgeous. No, I'm serious, you looked like an angel." Holden put her hand over the tiny mouthpiece and whispered, "Jennifer." The younger members of the table made a low, appreciative sound. Everyone over forty stared blankly. "Definitely the white. It's perfect for you. Well, don't let them talk you into it if it isn't what you want. Do you want me to call them? I'll do it. Perfect. Don't even think about it. Much love." She snapped the phone shut.

"They can call you any time?" George asked.

"It's relentless. That's why I had to find a place that I could really get away to, a place where no one can find me. Mother, I bought a little place in Cap Ferret while I was in Cannes, and you have to come there with me and we'll relax. It's very small, but it's right on the water, and when you open the windows in the bedroom, there is nothing in the world to want, *rien du tout*."

"*Comment puis-je m'y rendre?*" Jack said.

The group stared at him as if he'd spoken perfect Cantonese instead of decent high-school French. Every bone in his body, every muscle and cell, seemed to lean in her direction. He looked at her like Stamp looked at her, like he was willing to jump and jump until he landed in her arms.

"Since when do you speak French?" Kay said.

"*C'est très facile,*" Holden said to Jack.

I served the cake and we sang an accelerated version of the birthday song over the lit candles before the phone rang again. Taffy waited and made a wish.

"Have you been to Atlanta yet?" Taffy said, touching her napkin to her lips.

"It's not on my itinerary." Holden smiled at Jack, who refilled her glass of champagne.

"Have you spoken to your father?"

"Not in a couple of weeks. There's nothing I need to talk to him about."

Taffy looked relieved. It was perhaps the nicest gift that Holden could have given her. For now, at least, she was taking sides. She was standing firmly in her mother's court even if she had been a little late in getting there.

"How long can you stay?" Taffy asked.

"I was going to ask that," Jack said.

Kay stabbed a potato with her fork a little too hard and we all heard the tines hit the plate.

"Just a couple of days. I'm here illegally. My secretary has strict orders not to tell anyone where I am, but I can only hold things off for so long. This is such a busy season. Everyone wants to get their deals wrapped up before the whole world vanishes for summer."

"Well, there's plenty of room," I said. "Henry and Charlie's room is free. No one in Hollywood will be looking for you there."

"I got a hotel room," Holden said. She pushed her hair back and I saw the bright diamond sitting on the perfect curve of her earlobe. "I'm already checked in. I didn't want to just show up and expect to have a place to stay."

"Then you'll just check out," Taffy said. "You have a place to stay."

Holden stretched and put her arm around her mother's shoulder. "I'm such an awful hotel rat. You can be perfectly demanding in hotels the way you can never be at home. I have to have the *Times* and my coffee in the morning, and they have a good gym downstairs. Sometimes when I've been traveling a lot, I'll check into a hotel for a few days in L.A. I get so used to being taken care of."

"I can't imagine you'd have a hard time finding someone to take care of you," Trey said. Kay looked at him and for a minute I thought he might be the next victim of her fork.

"What a sweet bunch of people you are," Holden said.

"Really," Taffy said. "I want you to stay here. I haven't seen you in so long. If you don't want to, then I'll get a room with you."

"They're all booked up," Holden said. "I made these reservations weeks ago." She leaned over and kissed Taffy. "I wouldn't miss your birthday."

Taffy looked a little disappointed, but she kept it to herself. It would be hard to have a daughter like Holden, one who was so successful and self-contained that she couldn't possibly give the slightest indication of needing you at all.

Holden hugged her mother. "We'll have so much time together. I'll be over first thing in the morning."

"Your mother has a job now. She might be busy," I said.

"You have a job? Are you going to stay here?"

"I'm here for a little while," Taffy said. "Until things get settled. Caroline is letting me teach at her dance studio."

"She's wonderful," I said. "All the students love her."

Holden, who was perfectly polished, was stopped by this information. For an instant everything that was Hollywood about her fell away and she touched her mother's cheek with the back of her hand. "You were always a wonderful dancer. Isn't she wonderful? I'm so proud of you."

"I'm hardly doing anything."

"You're doing everything," she whispered. "I'm so sorry about all of this. I want to go to Atlanta and kill Daddy."

"He may already be dead," Taffy said. "I haven't been able to get him on the phone all week."

After the cake we all went into the living room and squeezed in two to a chair or sat on the floor.

"That was divine," Holden said. "Better than Campanile's."

"Erica's never seen *Tap*," George announced.

"What's *Tap*?" Trey said.

"You haven't seen *Tap*? Where have you people been? It's like saying you've never seen *An American in Paris*."

"I've never seen *An American in Paris*," Erica confessed.

"That makes two again," Trey said.

"Oh God," Kay said. "I feel an evening of tap dancing coming on."

"Everybody in my room," George announced. "I've got the tapes."

"Let's go over to my house," Trey said. "I've got a great television. What do you say, Jack? Feel like a little tap dancing?"

Jack rocked his head back and forth like he was trying to make up his mind. "Hmm, tough call, but no, no thank you. I've already seen them both. Still, if you and Erica plan to bond with the McSwains, you'll have a lot of tap-dancing films to work your way through, so you might as well get started now."

"It could be a late night," Erica said to her father.

"You have a key," Woodrow said. He kissed his lovely daughter and let her go off with my son.

While everyone said their good nights, Jack came and stood next to Holden. "Tap-dancing films?" he said.

"I've seen them all."

"Puis-je vous inviter à prendre un verre ce soir?"

"Vous?" She laughed.

He shrugged. *"Tu."*

"That's much more inviting."

Kay stood and stared while Trey went to get Holden's purse. "I don't even know what he asked her."

"He asked her for a drink," I said. I knew a little more than ballet French, and this

209

wasn't exactly a complicated exchange. A person could more or less figure out what was going on without speaking any language at all.

"A drink!" she said. "Is he insane?"

"No," I said, kissing her forehead good night, "but I think you might be. Go watch tap-dancing films with your fiancé. Have a good time."

Holden and Jack were halfway to the car. I heard the sheep bleat again, but I did not hear her answer the call.

When they were gone, it was just the grown-ups left — Taffy and Woodrow, Tom and me. We picked up glasses and plates for a while and then abandoned them to sit in the living room.

"That's some daughter you have," Woodrow said to Taffy.

"Look who's talking," she said, refilling her glass. There was a slug of room-temperature champagne left in the bottle on the coffee table. "There was a time in my life when I was Holden."

"You looked a lot like Holden at that age," Tom said.

"That's not even what I'm talking about," Taffy said. "I was *like* Holden. What's really so awful about being fifty-eight —" She stopped and looked at me, pointing a finger. "And *you*, keep your mouth shut. What's really so awful about being fifty-eight is that you don't ever have that experience again. Holden's got it and she probably doesn't even know it. No, I take that back: She knows it, but she doesn't understand that she isn't always going to have it."

"Excuse me," Tom said. "But what are you talking about?"

"I'm talking about men, the attention of men, the feeling you get when you walk in the room and you know that everybody has his eyes on you, bottom line, that everybody wants to sleep with you."

I slipped off my shoes and tucked my feet beneath me on the sofa. I didn't exactly feel comfortable talking about it, but I knew what she meant.

"And you feel like you don't have that anymore?" Woodrow said.

"I know I don't. Holden and I go to a restaurant now and I might as well be the coat she's carrying. The maître d' gives us the best table, the waiter comps her wine, all eyes are on our table, and no one is looking at me. And I'm not saying I blame her. She's my own daughter, I'm proud of her, I think everyone *should* be looking at her, but it reminds me of the way people used to look at me. Or it reminds me that they don't look at me that way anymore."

"You don't know what you're talking about," Tom said.

"Oh, I do, too. There was a time women

wouldn't leave their husbands alone with me. I may have been a flirt, but I was never a cheat, and still they wouldn't have let their husbands follow me out to the kitchen to get a drink. Now that's all changed. When I left Atlanta my friend Patty said, 'I'll have Richard drive you up to Raleigh. That's too far for you to drive by yourself. Ten hours in a car!' It's like being an old rottweiler with no teeth."

"But you're gorgeous. There isn't a woman your age in the world who looks better than you," I said.

"But you're including the key phrase, 'your age.' I look great for my age, but that doesn't make any difference. Men aren't interested in women my age. They're interested in women Holden's age. Hell, her father is out there right now doing the mambo with Miss Junior Executive on my birthday. For all I know, they're talking about having kids, making a nice little second family, but this time, he swears, he'll really be there. He'll do it right."

"You can't speak for all men," Tom said.

"That's right," Woodrow said.

"It's my birthday and I can speak for whomever I damn well please. You're good guys. You stayed with your wives, but if you were single, who could say?"

"I am single," Woodrow said. "I can say I like women my own age."

"You never went out with a woman twenty years younger than you?"

"Hell, I've got a daughter who's twenty years younger than me. I wouldn't be messing around with that."

"Well, that makes one. Neddy can date someone who's younger than Holden, but when I say to that young lawyer, Jack, You can be my date tonight, he's only too happy to help me out because to him it's *funny*. It's a joke. 'I'm going to pretend I'm with this old woman here.' He doesn't think I still have sex. He doesn't even think I think about it anymore. Women my age are out of the game. I just want to walk down the street one more time and have some guy turn around and look at my ass. It's a kind of power. I never realized at the time. Maybe you don't feel like you've got too much power in your life, but when somebody wants you, well, then you're something." The room had gone quiet. We all just sat there and looked at our drinks. "For God's sake, this is not my imagination. Back me up here, Caroline."

I sighed. "It's true," I said. "I wish I still got seated at the front of a restaurant."

"And?" Taffy said.

I hated this. I didn't want to say it in front of Woodrow and I really didn't want to say it in front of Tom, who was a good husband and always made me feel attractive. "Dammit.

All right, you're right, is that what you want me to say? I'm only going to admit it because it's your birthday. I wish some guy on the street would check out my ass." I put down my glass and hid my face in my hands. "How can I say that? The whole time I was young I was mortified when men stared at me, and once they stopped I started to miss it. What kind of feminist does that make me?"

"The honest kind," Taffy said, and finished her drink.

After that we were all ready to call it a night. Woodrow stayed and helped us clean up the kitchen even though we all tried to send him home. "I want you to work in my house," I said. "I just don't want you to load the dishwasher."

"Don't worry about it," he said. "I'll be back." He crouched down on the floor and Stamp came out from under the table and sat beside him. "Shake." He held out his hand and Stamp gave him his paw with dog solemnity.

"When did he learn how to do that?" Taffy said.

"He's always known how to do that. Hey, is it my imagination or is the dog getting fat?"

"It's nervous eating," I said, handing a cluster of glasses to Tom. "He misses you."

Woodrow stood up and stretched. "Then I should go before I wear out my welcome."

Taffy went and got Woodrow's jacket, which he had abandoned in the living room. "Happy birthday," he said, and handed her the present.

She looked at the package and touched the ribbon. "You didn't have to do that."

"It's for both of you," he said, looking at Stamp.

Taffy sat down and carefully peeled off the paper. It was something that drove me crazy about her when we were kids. She never tore into anything. She always slid her nail under the tape and pulled it apart in such a way that you could use the paper again if you wanted to, which we never did. At Christmas I had completely finished opening all of my presents before Taffy was finished with her first one. *You CAN Train Your Dog!* She held up the book. "Thank you. We'll read it together in bed."

"I'd like that." He waved to us.

"Come back soon," Tom said. "If you don't come back soon, my birthday is going to be moved to next week."

"I'll be here." Woodrow was slow to leave, and when he got out the door, he opened it again before it was all the way closed. "You want to have dinner with me next week?" he said to Taffy.

"What?"

"Don't make me ask twice," he said. "There are other people here."

215

She waved at him with her dish towel. "Get out of here. You're just feeling sorry for me because I made such a scene in the living room."

"You can say no, but don't say no for that reason."

She looked at him. Tom and I got busy at the sink and a plate slipped through my hands and shattered on the floor. I gave out a completely unnecessary yell. Taffy jumped about a foot.

"Well, good night again," Woodrow said.

"No," she said. "Wait a minute. Yes, I want to say yes, but I've got to ask you a question first."

"Shoot."

"You never call me by my name. When I met your daughter, she said you always called me Caroline's sister."

I thought it was a ridiculous prerequisite question for a date, but Woodrow stopped and scratched the back of his head. He was stalling. "Honestly? I just have a hard time calling a grown woman Taffy."

"Everybody has always called me Taffy."

"But is it your name?"

"Actually, no," she said, trying to put a little dignity into her voice, "my name's Henrietta, but I don't have the slightest idea what your name is either, unless it's Woodrow Woodrow."

"It's Felix."

I looked at him. "Felix?" I said.

"Like the cat?" Taffy said.

"Exactly. Like the cat."

"Not a great name. It might be worse than Henrietta, but it might be a toss-up — what do you think?"

"I think I didn't think this through very carefully when I brought it up in the first place and that I should call you whatever you want."

"Taffy," Taffy said.

"Woodrow," Woodrow said.

Taffy thought about it for a minute and then she nodded. "So, dinner next week."

Woodrow smiled. "We'll figure out a time."

"You know where I live," she said.

"I know where you live," he said, and he shut the door.

chapter twelve

The next morning Taffy was the first one up. When I came into the kitchen, she was sitting in her bathrobe with her feet up in the chair. "I have a date," she said.

"I know you do."

"I have a date with your black contractor."

"That's what it's looking like."

"You have to wonder what Neddy would say about that."

"Well, up until last night I would have wondered what you would have said about it. I hope you're not going to go out with him to gall Neddy. Woodrow's too good for that."

"We call him Felix."

"Don't be mean, Henrietta."

"Felix the contractor, wedding planner, dog trainer." She was laughing and then she stopped. "You know, I really do think he's a nice man. I can't say I'd marry him, but I want to have dinner with him."

"It's important to take these things one step at a time."

"God, I haven't been on a date in a really, really long time."

"You can borrow some of my clothes."

"Then he'll never ask me out again." Taffy looked at her watch. "I wonder what time Holden is going to get up. I wish I could call her now. She may be completely exhausted. Don't you think she looked good?"

"She's gorgeous. Everybody loved her."

"I never get to see Holden at all. Sometimes I feel like one more desperate actress trying to get her attention."

"Well, take the day off from work. I'll teach your classes. You and Holden can go paint the town."

"Really? I'd love that."

"That's the good thing about having your sister as a boss. You can always get the day off."

It was strange to teach Taffy's classes. It had been less than two weeks and already the girls seemed to have improved by two levels. After I went through all the regular routines, they said they wanted their new steps and that the other Mrs. McSwan (because we were sisters, it only stood to reason to the eight-year-old mind that we would have the same name) always taught them at least one new step every class. I showed them running flap heels, but they already knew running flap heels. I showed them the six-riff walk, but they acted like it was something they'd picked up in preschool. Finally I relented and gave them the whole Shuffle Off to Buffalo. They were thrilled with that. Over and over they shuffled to one side of the room and then back to the other. I wondered if Taffy would be disappointed. She was probably saving Shuffle Off to Buffalo for Christmas.

Taffy was disappointed, wildly so, and it had nothing to do with dancing. When I looked up, she was standing at the door waving an envelope in my direction. Her eyes were red from crying. At first I thought she must have been served with divorce papers, but the envelope looked awfully small.

"Keeping shuffling, girls," I said. "Back and forth." I hurried over to my sister at the door.

"I decided to go over to the hotel and see if she was up yet. The desk clerk gave me this."

She handed me a piece of hotel stationery and I took out the note and read it.

Dear Mother,

I'm sorry not to phone you, but it is so terribly early. I just got a call and I have to go to Rome to set up production on a picture. I have no life! I am so disappointed, but at least I got to be with you on your birthday. I know this may sound crazy, but Kay's friend Jack has decided to come with me and borrow my place in Cap Ferrat. We stayed up late last night talking and we both thought it sounded like fun. I think he was due for a vacation. I will call you soon!

Much love,
Holden

"That," I said, but then really didn't know what else to say. It was her daughter, after all. "That is really something."

Taffy snatched the note back and stuffed it into the envelope. "As if things weren't bad enough before. It would have been better if she'd never come at all."

"You don't mean that."

"Of course I mean that. Before Holden came to town, I could at least comfort myself by thinking about how great she'd turned out."

"Holden is great." I tried to make my voice sound convincing.

Taffy raised the envelope. "This is not the work of a great person. Jesus, Minnie, where did I go so wrong? You have Tom and four perfect kids, and I wind up with Neddy and Holden. I must have done something really horrible at some point. I have a completely rotten family."

"Listen to me. First off, I am your family, and so are Tom and my children, so you're fine on the family front. Second, my children are not perfect. Third, Holden is thirty-six years old. If she does something questionable, that is not a reflection on you as a mother. She's all grown up now. She makes her own decisions."

"It certainly looks that way." Taffy pressed the envelope to her forehead, and for a minute she looked like a clairvoyant trying to guess the contents of the letter even though she knew exactly what it said.

"Mrs. McSwan?" A little blond pixie named Laney stood on her right foot and then rested her left foot on top of her right. "Mrs. McSwans?"

"Yes," Taffy and I said.

"We're tired of Shuffling to Buffalo."

I had blocked out the methodical drum of tap shoes going across the floor.

"You taught my class to Shuffle Off to Buffalo?" Taffy said.

"You had already taught them everything else."

"Dammit," Taffy said. "You shouldn't have done that. I had an order planned."

"You shouldn't say that word," Laney said, her voice so quiet it could barely be heard above the pulsing shoes. I had a deep suspicion that Laney had been cutting her own bangs.

"You didn't tell me."

"I'll finish out the class," Taffy said.

"Forget about it. Just go home and try to relax. You don't need to deal with this."

When she turned to me, her neck was long

and her shoulders were back. Everything about her looked ready for a fight. "If they're going to Shuffle Off to Buffalo today, I might as well get some pleasure out of it." Taffy reached down and pulled her sweater over her head. She had come dressed for class. She must have stopped by the house after she got the letter and put her leotard on. That was how I knew she was really a dancer.

It was just as well that Taffy showed up to teach because when I went home I checked my calendar and there was a note that said: "Lunch with Kay, Mrs. Bennett, Mrs. Carlson, 1 o'clock." There was no part of me that believed I was capable of forgetting such a thing, but somehow I had, like people who don't remember certain horrific events of their childhood until thirty years later when a therapist pries it out of them under hypnosis. This lunch constituted my first suppressed memory. I tried to talk about my anxieties with Stamp, but he would have none of me. I think he must have gotten the news about Holden. The dog was in a terrible funk. The love of his life was off in the Eternal City with a D.A. who had no clean shirts. Which reminded me, I would have to break the news to Kay.

I really had to wonder about Jack. After all, Kay was a hometown girl. They had studied together in school. If they had developed some sort of long-term, lightweight attachment to each other that she was finding it difficult to give up, well, maybe that was understandable. Stupid, but understandable. But Holden was a player. She'd dated men who had been on the cover of *Rolling Stone*, she'd dated a guy who wrote for *Rolling Stone*, and once, for five days that the entire family would just as soon forget about, she dated one of the Rolling Stones. This girl — and in saying this I by no means cast aspersions on her sexual purity — had been around. Why would she fall for some rumpled-up county employee with a good smile and a mediocre French accent? Wouldn't she be impervious to that by now? Wouldn't she be impervious to just about everything? Was this guy so fantastic that it would be worth devastating her mother at the time of her divorce? The question, when all was said and done, was this: Was Holden that bad or was Jack that good?

When I went into my closet, I remembered that I wasn't supposed to wear my own clothes to these things, but honestly, since I would soon be revealed as a total fraud, I might as well break the truth out in stages. Better that they would hear my story of middle-class poverty while I was wearing the pair of nice slacks and the loose top that I had worn to nearly every symphony and dance recital for the last five years, than to hear me tell the tale in one of my sister's Chanel suits. And I was bound and determined to tell it, to all of them together, today. But first there was the issue of Jack. I called Kay at the office and asked if she would pick me up. "And come early. I want to talk about something before the lunch."

"Is everything okay?" she asked.

"Sure. Everything's fine." I headed off for a shower, hoping this would be the case.

When Kay arrived she was clutching two pieces of moss-green fabric, one satin, one chiffon. "I keep going over this," she said. "And I think the blue is so gorgeous, but I think the green really says more about me. Don't you think it's a more individualistic color?"

I looked at it. Not so individualistic if you were moss. "Sure."

"You like it?"

"I do."

"Do you love it?"

Kay, I wanted to scream at her, baby, it's *fabric,* open your eyes, but I tried to bear in mind the whole Big Day element of this that had escaped me. "Love it."

"I love it," she said.

"And Trey?"

"What about him?"

"Do you love him?"

"Oh, Mother, if this is about me bringing

Jack to the party last night, you just have to forget about it. Jack is a friend. I guess I've enjoyed his company a lot over the years, and we both feel bad thinking that we won't be spending as much time together in the future. Even once the wedding plans really get going, there won't be any time left over for Jack, so I think it's only natural we'd want to do some things together now. I mean, we'll still be good friends after the wedding. Trey doesn't mind me having friends who are men. But I'm not going to kid myself. I know it will be different."

I sat down and patted the place on the sofa next to me. "Sit down."

Kay sat down, the fabric still in her hand.

"Holden left the country this morning. She had to go to Rome."

Kay rolled her eyes. "Isn't that just like her? I mean, she's fabulousness itself and everything, but don't you think that's awfully selfish? First she doesn't come to see Taffy after the split, and then she shows up unannounced, dominates the entire party, and then blows out of town without spending any time with her mother. I bet she didn't even call. I bet she just left her a note."

"That's right."

"Poor Taffy, that's all I can say. She deserves better than that."

I touched Kay's engagement ring and automatically she smiled. It was like scratching

Stamp in that spot that made his back leg kick uncontrollably. Any attention that was paid to her ring delighted her, and I wanted to delight her. I wanted her to focus on happiness and Trey and the fact that they were getting married. There was a chance that this other piece of news was going to mean nothing to her at all. "There's one more thing."

"Let me guess. She didn't pay her hotel bill."

"Jack went with her."

Kay's eyes opened until they resembled nothing as much as two blue marbles. "That slut! He went with her to the hotel last night?"

I smiled a little at this. I shouldn't have but I did. I wasn't sure if she was attaching the word *slut* to Holden or Jack. "Probably. Yes, I think you could count on it, but that's not what I'm talking about. He went with her to Rome."

"What do you mean he went with her to Rome?"

"I mean Jack traveled with Holden to Rome."

"Jack didn't have plans to go to Rome."

"Honey, you're not getting this. Jack and Holden — we used to call it running off together. There may be a more modern term for it now."

Her eyes stayed big and they never left my

eyes. It didn't start in her eyes, anyway. It started in her hands. They were shaking and she folded them together. The wave of shaking moved up like a seismic chart during an earthquake. Her stomach trembled, her chest began to sway, her shoulders rocked forward and back. By the time it reached her neck, she was red and her mouth was open, both lips pulling and shaking in complete independence from each other. Her nose twitched twice and then she started to cry. She pitched straight forward into my lap and she let out one long, horrible wail of the kind I had not heard her make since her prom date stood her up her senior year of high school, the long, baleful moan of a seal who has just watched her cub being clubbed to death on the ice. This was very bad. This was worse than anything I could have put together in a worst-case scenario. I petted her hair, her beautiful hair. I could feel the hot dampness of her tears as they seeped through my pants and spread out across my thigh. I rubbed circles on her heaving back while she cried and cried and cried. So she really had loved Jack. It was Jack she had wanted to marry all along. He wouldn't even be in Rome yet. For all I knew, he was sitting in some American airport with Holden right now, holding hands, waiting to board their first-class seats on their connecting flight. I surreptitiously glanced at my watch. We still had an hour before lunch, which would be cutting it extremely close when you took into account time to get through the entire sobbing cycle, get fixed up again, drive across town, and find a parking space. "Do you think you can talk about this?" I asked, hoping to move things along a little. There was only more crying, not even a recognition that she had heard me, which maybe she hadn't. Despite the fact that I believe Kay had royally screwed things up, I really did feel for her, both because a mother cannot help but feel for her child when she is in this much pain, but also because I guess I could imagine her scenario of wanting Jack and thinking that he would come through for her before it was too late. It wasn't an honorable plan, but it was human.

"Kay," I said softly, hooking her hair behind her ears so she would hear me. "I think we should cancel lunch." What I meant, of course, was that I thought we should cancel the wedding, but she would have to be the one to say those words.

She sat up. Kay never used to wear mascara. She said it wasn't made for people with soft hearts, but she had started wearing it since her engagement as part of her larger effort to fix herself up. Now she looked like a girl who had just come up from the coal mines, and my pants and shirt were so utterly ruined, I could only be grateful that I hadn't borrowed anything from Taffy. "We can't cancel lunch," she said. "Mrs. Carlson and Mrs. Bennett will be there."

"Do you really want to go through with this?" I left the *this* indefinite.

Kay nodded and I went off to find a box of Kleenex. When I came back and handed it to her, she pulled up five. "How could they have done that to me? How could they have just left together like that? They knew this was my time." She looked at me. "It's supposed to be *my* time."

"I'm not quite sure I'm following you."

"When a person gets married, nobody is supposed to go to Rome." She laughed a little while crying. She hadn't meant for it to come out that way exactly.

"Are you in love with Jack?"

"Oh, hell. I don't know. I am and I'm not. But he said he loved me. He said he was going to change my mind. He didn't even care." Again she was crying.

"So what if he didn't care? You're marrying someone else." I suddenly felt my well of sympathy trickling away, the milk of human kindness soaking into a stone-dry creek bed. "I can't say I had a whole lot of respect for Holden and Jack flying off to Rome, but that's because it's thoughtless to Taffy, not because it's thoughtless to you."

"How can you say that?" Kay asked. She leaned away from me and got more tissue.

"It's horrible for me."

"What was Jack supposed to do, pine after you through your whole engagement, come to the church screaming, 'No, stop!' and carry you off in your big white wedding dress while everyone watched?"

"He said he would do that," she said.

I loved Kay, I swear to God, I loved her, and at the same time I wanted to slap her into next week. "And what was Jack supposed to do if you never relented? Is he supposed to waste his time feeling rotten so you can get your ego needs met? And what about Trey if you run off with Jack? You want to humiliate him and his family, break his heart just because it was the only way you could get Jack to marry you? Or did you want to have them both? These are good men, Kay, and you're a good woman, but you don't get to have them both."

"I just hadn't decided," she said quietly.

I picked up her hand, maybe a little too roughly. "You *did* decide. There's your proof. You picked. You said yes. If you made the wrong choice, then be a decent person and give Trey his ring back so he can get on with his life. Then if you want to, you can get on a plane to Rome and fight your cousin for the man you love." I stood up and tossed her Kleenex box on the couch. "I'm going to change clothes. If you still want to have lunch, you better get ready fast."

"I was never like Holden," Kay said as I was walking away.

I turned to hear her out.

"I was never the girl that the guys really wanted. I was just okay. I was the second choice, the best friend, the backup if their date fell through. Jack could never make up his mind about me until I made up my mind about someone else. And you know what? It was great. The two smartest, best-looking guys both wanting to marry me." She looked at me, her face awash in black tears. "It was great."

"Well, I'm glad you had some fun, but you're not in junior high school now. You're thirty years old and you're a lawyer and these are both good men. I won't say they deserve better than you, because I still think you're a wonderful woman, but they sure do deserve to be treated better than you're treating them. Now either call Mrs. Bennett and cancel, or wash your face and let's go."

I was furious with Kay even though I understood her being upset that Jack was gone. I tried to decide if I would have been this angry if it weren't for all the hell we had gone through trying to figure out how to get the money for this wedding. Maybe I wouldn't have been so angry if Neddy hadn't just stopped calling Taffy, or if Holden hadn't turned out to be such a beautiful disappointment. People should be a little more decent to each other.

We drove in silence to the restaurant, neither one of us willing to give in, or maybe Kay had given in but she was just too cried out to talk about it. We were meeting at the country club, which was old, venerable, and white, white, white, except, of course, for everyone who worked there. It was a place that Tom and I avoided like the plague and the place where Kay and Trey were having their reception, if they were getting married. I knew one thing for sure, this wasn't the day I was going to bring up our money problems.

Mrs. Bennett and the woman I took to be Mrs. Carlson were already seated in the dining room when we arrived. Mrs. Carlson was a very thin woman in her forties who wore a kelly-green suit and a diamond-crusted pin of a bumblebee on her shoulder, as if the insect had just lighted there and spontaneously petrified into jewels. I was in a bad mood. Introductions were made.

"Kay, darling," Mrs. Bennett said. "Are you all right?"

"I have a cold," Kay said quietly.

"She has a cold and she came anyway. Now, that's devotion for you. If we were anywhere close to the wedding, I'd be upset with you for making yourself sicker, but you have plenty of time to recover. The wedding is still a year away."

"Trey and I haven't decided yet."

Lila Bennett gave me a sad look as if I had failed her. "We have to work on that. Have you picked the color?"

Kay said something inaudible.

"Pardon me?"

"Moss," Kay said, the word barely eking out of her throat. If she had been a child, I would have taken her into the ladies' room and told her to pull herself together. Instead we received our leather-bound menus and ordered. Kay chose the consommé.

"You'll need more than that if you're going to keep your strength up," Mrs. Carlson said. Mrs. Carlson who clearly had never eaten more than a bowl of consommé in her life.

Mrs. Bennett put her hand over Kay's wrist and squeezed. "It's such a stressful time. Such a happy time, a joyful time, but people forget how hard it is, too, especially on the bride."

Get your hands off my daughter, I wanted to say. It's my job to comfort her, and right now she doesn't deserve to be comforted. I seriously doubted such a speech would have been helpful to anyone.

Mrs. Carlson took out a notebook and uncapped her Mont Blanc. "There are so many details, thousands of details that go into a fine wedding. It's more than any person could manage by themselves. I know that you and Mrs. Bennett have both been married a very long time. You probably don't even remember all that went into your own weddings."

"I remember it all," I said.

Mrs. Bennett smiled. "As do I. It was the happiest day of my life."

The happiest day? Not by a long shot. It was a perfectly fine day, but it didn't even come into the running when I thought of the birth of my children, their grade-school pageants, their graduations. It didn't compare to the opening of my school. It didn't come close to a thousand days I'd spent with Tom since our silly little wedding, days we raked up leaves, or played a hand of gin in bed before we went to sleep, or listened to a Chet Baker record with the lights off and then went to our room upstairs and made love. Nobody could tell me you could put a wedding up against any of that. "I eloped," I said.

Mrs. Bennett and Mrs. Carlson looked at each other. *Elopement* was only a word they'd spelled out in crossword puzzles. "That must have been very Bohemian," Mrs. Carlson said.

I shrugged. "It seemed like the thing to do at the time."

Mrs. Carlson nodded and went back to her notes. "So I'll assume you won't be wearing your mother's dress. There isn't really much we can do until two certain people pick a date. The ballroom here is very much in demand. I have a list of availabilities, and I think you'll see there isn't even anything there within six months." She handed the paper to Kay, who took it with trembling hands. "Everything comes down to the dates, the flowers you choose, the cut of your dress, even your colors. The moss, for example, wouldn't be right for summer."

"It would be so lovely to marry in the summer," Mrs. Bennett said.

"But that doesn't mean there aren't things to be done today. Numbers, for example. Kay, have you and Trey made up your lists for bridesmaids and groomsmen?"

I could see the weeping coming up again, the subtle movement in the corners of Kay's mouth, the dampness of her forehead, and all of a sudden I wasn't angry with her anymore. I would never be angry enough at her to let her bear the humiliation of falling apart in the country club in front of people she longed to impress. "Do you need to go?" I said softly.

Kay nodded her head with no more than an inch of movement. I stood up immediately. "I am extremely sorry," I said. "I told her we should cancel the lunch, but she wouldn't do it. Kay really is feeling bad."

"If you're feeling bad, then go," Mrs. Bennett said, a genuine kindness in her voice that surprised me. "All of this can be done later."

"I'm so sorry," Kay whispered.

"There is nothing to be sorry about." And then Mrs. Bennett did something that I found both odd and very touching. She picked up Kay's hand and she kissed it. "Go home with your mother and she'll put you to bed."

"I'll do just that," I said. I pulled back Kay's chair and she leaned on my arm as I walked her out of the dining room.

"I should be shot," Kay said, looking out the window at the line of Mercedeses and Lexuses as we pulled through the parking lot of the country club.

"It's not as bad as that."

"I've gotten very, very confused." She touched her diamond ring. "I need to go home and get things straightened out in my head."

"It may be a good thing that Jack's gone," I said to her.

"That's the question, because it's either a good thing or the worst thing I can think of."

237

chapter thirteen

Taffy would not get off the phone. She called Holden's secretary at least ten times the first day. "You do know where she is. I even know where she is. She's in Rome setting up a production for a film, and since it's a film, I assume it's business, and if it's business, I assume you know where she is. Now, if you know where she is and you're not telling me because she's told you not to tell anybody, then I want to remind you that I'm her mother. . . . Well, do you have her number in Cap Ferret? Ferret. Like the weasel but with a better pronunciation. She bought a house there. Well, she has a cell phone. There were cell phones in France the last time I checked. Holden hasn't gone out of the house without a cell phone since they were invented. . . . Yes, fine, you do that, but I'll call back again. I may not know how to get ahold of her, but I know how to get ahold of you, and I will continue to do that until you locate her for me. . . . Good, then we understand each other."

She pushed down the button and dialed again.

"Neddy? Neddy, if you're there, pick up the phone. This is not about me and it's not about Buddy Lewis. This is about Holden. Call me back."

"What difference does it make? What are you going to do if you find her?" I said.

"I'm going to make her come back here. It isn't right. You don't show up and then disappear with some guy you just met. I need to talk to her."

"So you talk to her and she says, Mom, I met a guy and I blew you off and I'm really sorry. Then what?"

"Minnie, I feel . . . I feel like everything is falling apart and I can't stop it. I can't make anything have order except for those little girls in their tap shoes. I just want someone to play fair, to be held accountable. I've had a very hard time coming to terms with the fact that my husband is a complete bastard. I don't want to have to think ill of my daughter, too. I want her to come home so I won't *have* to think ill of her."

She got out the white pages and started flipping through.

"Do you think she's still in Raleigh?"

"Be quiet. Here, let me have your glasses." I handed her my glasses and she looked at the phone book again and dialed the number. "Jack Carroll, please."

"You know he's not there."

She waved me off. "Out of the office? Do

you have a number where he can be reached? Yes, it is important. This is the U.S. Attorney General's office. I'm holding a file on Jack Carroll in my hands. We're reopening a case of his."

"Taffy, put down the phone."

"No, I will not speak to someone in the department. Jack Carroll was the lawyer on the case. Don't tell me you let your A.D.A.s leave without a forwarding number. . . . Do you know when he'll be back?"

I leaned over and hung up the phone.

"What in the hell are you doing?" she said.

"When they trace this call, and they will, it's going to look pretty suspicious that it's coming from the public defender's home number, don't you think?"

"I'll call back from a pay phone."

"You're insane."

She was dialing again. "Margaret? Hello there, it's Mrs. Bishop. I've been fine, and you? . . . No, just out of town for a while. Visiting my sister in Raleigh . . . Yes, it is lovely here . . . Does she? Your cousin. No, I didn't know that. Is Mr. Bishop — . . . Now that you mention it, he did say something about a trip. You know me, scatterbrain. Do you have the number? No number? Fiji? Are you sure? You think I would have remembered Fiji. Margaret, I have such a little question, do you know what? I think Ilena McNeal could help me. If you could transfer me to — Really. Now, that's bad luck. And you don't know when she'll be back in town? I'll tell you what, let me leave my number. Then when you hear from one of them, you can have them call me. Thank you. Yes. Good to talk to you, too."

She hung up and rested her head against the receiver. "I swear to God the room is spinning. I am going to be completely, permanently sick. Fiji. Now I'm going to have to track him down in Fiji."

"You'd be a natural in the FBI," I said.

"The FBI. Does Tom have any friends in the FBI? Maybe someone he went to law school with a million years ago?"

"Not that I can think of. Who is Ilena McNeal?"

"Who do you think she is?" Taffy didn't look up at me.

"God, you know everything."

"I know everything except where Holden is. There has to be a way to find her."

"You could get on a plane to Rome. I hear it's a great city to walk around in."

"Too many cats. Besides, I'm not even sure she's in Rome."

"I'm glad you were the one who said it."

"How's Kay doing? Has there been any progress on the wedding front?"

"I think everything's on ice while Kay recovers from her mysterious imaginary virus. She can only hold them off for so long. She's not even being very careful. Tom said he caught her sneaking into the office. Trey called me yesterday to see how she was really feeling. She told him not to come over, she says she doesn't want to give him anything."

"My, that's certainly metaphoric."

"He's probably been trying to call again today and just can't get through, in which case I thank you for tying up the line. I don't like to lie to Trey. He seems like someone who has no concept of lying." I looked at my watch. "Isn't it time for you to go to school, or do you want me to take your class?"

Taffy sighed and pushed herself up from her chair. "No, it will do me good to go and boss the short people around. I can pretend I'm their mother and make them do everything I say."

"The nice thing about dance students: They do everything you say, they go home at the end of the hour, and they pay you."

George was there when I came in from the grocery store. I had almost forgotten he still lived at home. Taffy had taken over his classes at the studio. Not only did I never see him, I never seemed to have time to think about him anymore. Because he had no messy, demanding problems, I had all but forgotten about him, my youngest son. When he took the grocery bags from me, I put my arms around him. "George!" I said. "My life! Where have you been?"

"I've been in the library and I've been in love."

I took a step back and looked up at him. George was tall. "Love?"

"Erica Woodrow, Erica Woodrow. How many times can I say it?"

"As many times as you want, I guess."

"I may be the surprise winner in this race. No one would suspect it, George coming up fast from behind."

"What are you talking about?"

"Kay's marriage, Taffy's divorce. I could beat them both."

"You want to marry Erica?"

"Like you can't believe."

"George, don't be ridiculous. You're twelve."

He was teasing me. I thought he was teasing me. He reached in the bag and took out a carrot, which he polished off (unwashed) in three bites. "I'm twenty-five, oh you who were married at twenty."

"God, I regret telling any of you that story. I am glad you're so happy. It's a relief to have someone happy around here."

"Well, Kay's happy, isn't she?"

"Boy, you *are* in love. You used to have your fingers on the pulse of this place. Jack the D.A. ran off to Rome with your cousin Holden."

George sat down in his chair. He set the leafy end of the carrot on the table and stroked it with his fingers thoughtfully. "Are you kidding me?"

"Nobody could make that up."

He shook his head. "That bastard."

I was rooting through the bags for frozen food. I had a tendency to get sidetracked while putting the groceries away, only to come back an hour later to a puddle of ice cream. "Why do you say that?"

"Because he snowed me. He made a big play to enlist me in his campaign to win back Kay. He said he was so in love with her that they were meant to be together. He thought Trey was all wrong for the part, and he needed me to help him. I liked the guy. I think I helped him."

"Maybe you should tell that to Kay. She's about as miserably confused as one person can be."

"I'll stop by her place on my way back to school. I think I was wrong about Trey, anyway. He's just such an easy target. He's too rich, he's too good looking, he's too nice. What's there to like? But when we went to his house to watch movies the other night, I started thinking I should have cut him a break. He made us popcorn, he got everybody a pillow. I don't know. He was so nice to Erica. I'm starting to suspect that underneath all that wealth and privilege there beats the heart of a really decent guy. I think I better go talk to Kay." George stood up and kissed me. "It was good to see you."

"Wait a minute, I don't know anything about you."

"I told you I'm in love. You know everything about me."

"Well, then, I don't know everything about Erica. Is she in love with you?"

George looked puzzled by my question, almost offended. "Of course she's in love with me."

"I know you're lovable, but sometimes these things are unevenly felt. I was just asking."

"You can't be in love like this unless the other person loves you."

"It certainly is more fun."

George looked in the bag and pulled out three cans of soup, which he took to the pantry. "Do you believe that for every person there's one person?" he asked over his shoulder.

His voice was so earnest it broke my heart. "Like a missing half? No, I guess I don't."

"I didn't, either." He came out of the pantry.

"And now you do?" There was a time I had been so good at reading my children, but now I was missing everything. Looking at George standing in front of me in the kitchen, really focusing on him for the first time since I don't know when, I could see a sheen of happiness covering his skin, the warm, pink happiness of a heart that beat more joyfully, more gratefully.

"I do, completely. Maybe there isn't one for everybody. I wouldn't know about that, but for me, yes."

"And you'd sign your name on the dotted line tomorrow, and she would, too?"

"Right here in this kitchen. This is the person I'm going to be looking at when I die."

My eyes filled up with tears and I had a sudden tightness in my throat. I never would have expected it. "How can you be sure?"

"There's no law, you just are. But you were sure, right? You and Dad were sure?"

I ripped off a paper towel and wiped my eyes. "I'm sure now, but back then? No, we were just young. We loved each other and we jumped in and swam like hell." I sat down in a kitchen chair. I felt like Kay. I felt as though I wanted to cry the Mississippi, cry until every bit of it had washed out of me. I took a deep breath and waited for the feeling to pass. "This is so funny, but I had almost the same conversation with your sister that night you brought Jack over. She asked me if I had been sure and I couldn't tell her the truth. I couldn't tell her because she wasn't sure. But for you it's different."

"Mom, certainly you know by now that

where Kay and I are concerned, it's always different."

I laughed. "You're a very lucky man."

"I'll tell you something. I love the law, and I love dancing. I feel like I'm comfortable with both, that I'm good at both. Either one would have been possible, but neither one was exactly a perfect fit, something I stepped into and said, Yes, this is who I am. But when I'm with Erica I *know*, this is who I am."

I nodded. That was the way I felt about dance. That was the thing that had been completely natural in my life. Once I strapped on my shoes, I felt completed, whole. I loved my marriage, my children, but I had had to work at those. Maybe George was right, maybe we each get one thing, our missing half, but maybe it isn't always a person.

"You've got to bring Erica over more. I want to see her when there aren't so many other people in the room."

"She'd like that."

"What about Woodrow? Does Woodrow know?"

George shrugged. "I think he gets it, I'm not really sure. He's building a garage outside of Chapel Hill right now. The commute is really wearing him out. I saw a lot more of Woodrow when I was hanging out at my house than I do when I hang out at his house."

"Well, I'm really happy for you. Whatever happens, I'm happy that you've had this experience."

George leaned over and kissed the top of my head. It was something I used to do to him when he was in his high chair and I was spooning creamed peas into his mouth. "You're not listening," he said quietly. "I already know what's going to happen."

Maybe love was in the ground, a colorless, odorless gas that lived in the bedrock and every now and then managed to dislodge itself from the earth and seep up through the soil, through the basement and the floorboards to fill up the house. Maybe we were infected, intoxicated, a whole house held under the invisible sway of love we could not see. Or maybe love was a virus that one person brought in from the cold, and then it passed from person to person until suddenly everyone was swaying to the low, jazzy beat they didn't know they heard. I should put a sign on the door that said WARNING! MARRIAGE WITHIN! ENTER AT YOUR OWN RISK.

Or maybe I should put a sign on the door that said COME INSIDE.

Taffy couldn't find Holden or Neddy, though she didn't stop trying. She taught her classes. A couple of times I caught her talking on the phone to Woodrow.

Kay nursed her mysterious illness. She said she was starting to feel better. Trey was bringing her cupcakes that he had made himself. Anyone who knew Kay knew that she was a fool for cupcakes.

The next morning when Tom and I came into the kitchen for breakfast, the coffee was already made, and Woodrow was there reading the paper. Stamp was asleep in his lap.

"You're back!" I said.

"Hey," Tom said. "I thought the rule was no dogs on the furniture."

"Do I look like furniture?" Woodrow said. He had one hand on Stamp's back and ran his thumb back and forth between the narrow shoulder blades.

"I thought you were building a garage?" I poured coffee for Tom and myself and then I refilled Woodrow's cup.

"I'm trying to spread myself around, make everybody a little bit happy instead of making anybody completely happy."

"I'd settle for that," Tom said.

"So did you know that our children are hopelessly in love with each other?" I asked.

"I hear about very little else." Woodrow leaned forward to get the milk, and Stamp shifted, sighed, and put his muzzle back down on Woodrow's knees.

"How do you feel about it?" Tom was asking him, one father to another. I was surprised, because I knew what he was saying, and somehow I thought it would be one of those things that, in our progressive household, would always be left unsaid.

"I never particularly liked the idea of my girls dating white men. It happened with the older girls once or twice. I never said anything about it, but in the end it always blew over and I was relieved. My three older girls married black men. I don't need to tell you, that's easier. In a hundred different ways it's easier. When you think about your children, you think life is going to be hard enough in ways you can't predict. There's no sense setting a tougher course for yourself right from the start."

It was true. Everything he said was true, but I thought he would have said, What are you talking about? I never even noticed.

"What Erica and George are doing now, they would have been killed for it in North Carolina, both of them. And not so long ago. We think we're such a progressive country. We take such a high moral ground with everybody else. But this isn't the Dark Ages I'm talking about. This was fifty years ago, maybe even forty years ago. Back then if they didn't kill you, they wouldn't hire you or rent to you or speak to you in church. Someone chooses that life, they're choosing something awfully hard."

"Aren't you the guy who asked my sister out?" I said.

He shrugged. "I'm sixty-three years old. Nobody gives a damn what I do. Anyway, I like your sister."

"And you like George," I said. How could Woodrow care? He couldn't possibly care. What was true for the rest of the world was not true for our families, for our children.

"Well, that's what makes it all okay. If Erica had come home with a white boy, I would have been worried for her, I can't deny that. But I don't think of George as a white boy. I think of George as George. I think of him as a friend of mine. I wish Erica hadn't fallen in love with a white boy, but I'm glad she's fallen in love with George, if that makes any sense."

"I think that makes all the sense in the world," Tom said. "Do you want scrambled eggs? I think today is the day I risk my heart on some eggs."

"Eggs wouldn't be bad," Woodrow said.

And that was that, the entire conversation about the racial lines that we'd spent our lives living inside of and fighting our way out of. A two-minute conversation punctuated by an egg.

Taffy walked into the kitchen in her bathrobe and slippers. For the first few weeks she was with us, she came to the breakfast table looking like she was on her way to Saks. But now her face was bare, her hair pushed back behind her ears. She looked up and saw

Woodrow. You could tell she was thinking about turning around, but she was already too far into the room to back out gracefully.

"Couldn't you emit some sort of high-pitched noise when you enter the house?" she said.

"I can, but it bothers the dog's ears."

"Well, so much for being mysterious." She padded over to the coffeepot and poured herself a cup. "Every woman dreads the moment a man sees her for the first time without makeup. At least we got it out of the way before the first date."

"Speaking of which —"

"If you back out at this particular moment, it will be very ungentlemanly of you."

"I was going to ask what night was good for you."

"I'll need to check my calendar," Taffy said with great seriousness. "But right off the top of my head? Let's see. Tonight, tomorrow night, any night this week or next week."

"Good. How about tonight?"

"Would you guys like a little privacy?" I said.

"No," they answered in unison.

"Tonight is good," Taffy said. "But now I really do need to take my coffee back into my room and close the door."

"Any word from Holden?"

"You know about that?"

"Erica told me."

Taffy shook her head. "I'm still working on it. So I guess I'll see you later."

"Seven?"

"Seven is good." She walked out of the room and then stuck her head back around the door. "This isn't some complicated plot about you wanting to get my dog away from me, is it?"

Stamp raised his head at the word *dog* and wagged his tail. "Yes," Woodrow said.

"As long as I know where I stand."

chapter fourteen

Usually I dance along with my girls, but today my hip was killing me. I remember some of the dance teachers I had when I was a child. They might have worn leotards, but they always just stood on the side of the room counting. One of them, Mrs. Leominster, used to smoke while she called out the steps. If they wanted to show us something, they only moved one foot, as if the foot was a separate thing with its own little piece of information to impart. I never thought it was right. I thought, One of these days I'm going to have a dance studio and I'm going to dance all day, I'll dance for every class I teach. I had, and I did, but today it was rainy and cold and everything in me was screaming out for a set of new plastic joints. It made me mad as hell when I couldn't get my body to go along with the program.

When I got home the house was bright and the smell of garlic and oregano rushed out into the night when I opened the door. Taffy was at the stove with a dish towel tied around her waist.

"Don't you have an apron?" she said.

I dropped my bag on the floor and came over to the stove. "I never use them."

"Now I know what to get you for Christmas."

"I thought you were going out to dinner?"

"I am going out to dinner but you're not. Here, taste this."

I took the spoon from her hand and tasted. It was rich and deep, tiny bits of carrot and zucchini and onion swimming in a dark broth. "I didn't know you could cook like this."

"Face it, you didn't know anything about me."

"What is it?"

She shrugged. "Chicken soup, chicken stew depending on how thick it gets."

"God, this is nice of you. Why don't you forget about going back to Atlanta? Send for the rest of your stuff, if you have any other stuff there, and move in. You can cook and teach."

"Are you offering me a role as an indentured servant?"

"I am."

Taffy took off the dish towel, and for the first time I noticed that she was wearing the same camel outfit she had on the day she showed up here. It struck me that she wanted to make a good impression on Woodrow, and that she must have wanted to make a good impression on us at the end of her long drive. "You look beautiful," I said.

She looked down at herself as if to see what I was talking about. "Really? Do you think so? I was wondering if I should wear a skirt."

"You're perfect."

Tom walked in carrying a scotch. "Can you believe this?" he said. "A gourmet meal, and she fixed me a drink, too." He kissed me and then he kissed Taffy. "It's like being married to sisters."

"I'm in a very low-grade good mood," Taffy said. "Don't get used to it."

The doorbell rang and immediately Taffy touched her hair.

"You're perfect," I told her again.

"The man who is sitting in my kitchen every morning reading the newspaper before I even get up is now ringing the doorbell. What is happening to the world?" Tom went to answer the door. "Good evening, sir," he said to Woodrow.

Woodrow came into the kitchen. He had on a red bow tie tonight with a blue shirt and a navy jacket. I thought he should run for president.

"Now before you start in," Taffy said to Tom and me, "let me tell you, there will be no jokes about 'Where are you taking our little girl?' or 'You better have her in by eleven' or 'You kids have fun.' Understood?"

"I had actually planned on making those jokes," I said. "Maybe not all of them, but at least one."

"There, I saved you the trouble."

"Can I get you a drink?" Tom asked Woodrow.

Woodrow shook his head. "I'm pretty much a one-drink man, so I'd just as soon have it in a restaurant if it's all the same to you."

Taffy got her purse. "So then, the soup is ready anytime you want it. Just don't let it boil."

Woodrow looked into the pot. "You made this?"

"She cooks," Tom said.

"Good night," Taffy said, clearly in a hurry to leave.

Once they were gone, Tom put his arms around my waist and kissed me. "So, George is gone."

"Correct."

"And there goes Taffy."

"Correct again."

"And we don't have to worry about dinner."

The doorbell rang.

"Maybe they forgot something," I said hopefully.

"You're dreaming."

It was Trey. He was bearing no flowers and his tie was off. "I'm so sorry for just showing up this way," he said. "I didn't even really know I was coming here. I was just driving around. You're getting ready to have dinner."

"We're having soup," Tom said. "Have some soup."

I was waiting for the polite refusal, but Trey pulled out a chair at the kitchen table and sat down. I doled out three bowls of soup while Tom got the silverware and the wine.

"It's gotten warm so quickly," Trey said. I wondered if that was what he had come to tell us. He didn't exactly seem dejected, but he seemed like he would be dejected if he were the kind of person to show his feelings.

"It'll do that," Tom said.

"Have you talked to Kay lately?"

"I talked to her today," I said. I had, but I had stopped asking her any questions. We just kept checking in with each other. She was trying to decide what to do. I knew that when she was ready to talk she would tell me so.

"Did she seem okay to you?"

"I think she's feeling better."

Trey ate a spoonful of soup and then put the spoon back in the bowl. "I'm afraid that Kay is going to call off the engagement."

I put down my spoon as well. Tom filled Trey's wineglass.

"What makes you say that?"

"The way she's been since Jack left with

her cousin. I think maybe she didn't realize she was in love with him until he was gone. I think he was the one she wanted to marry."

"Kay doesn't want to marry Jack," Tom said.

I was a little surprised that he answered, especially that he answered the way he did. Tom usually left everything in the emotional realm to me.

Trey, momentarily comforted, ate some more soup. "What makes you say that?"

"She doesn't love him. She loves you. Jack was a smooth talker, a real D.A. Maybe she got confused by all the flash, but trust me, if you've got the patience to hang on a little longer, Kay's going to come out of her fog."

I was floored. Where had Tom gotten this? He said it with such authority that even I wondered if it was true.

"Do you really think so?" Trey asked.

"Absolutely."

"Mrs. McSwain, Caroline, do you think he's right?"

Tom looked at me, told me with complete visual accuracy what my answer should be. I had to trust him on this one. "I'm sure of it."

Trey put his head in his hands and for a minute I thought he was going to start weeping.

"The question is, Can you wait for her to

see it for herself?" Tom said.

Trey looked up, first at Tom and then at me. "Of course I can wait. What choice do I have? I'm in love with her."

Trey finished his soup, thanked us profusely, and sought our forgiveness for interrupting our dinner, though we reassured him that he had done no such thing. I wasn't sure of anything, but I thought he was leaving our house a happier man.

"What in the world was that about?" I asked Tom.

"He's a smart guy," Tom said. "He figured things out."

"I don't mean with him, I mean with you. Why did you tell him that?"

"In the business we call it buying your client some time."

"You were buying Kay time?"

"Exactly." Tom refilled our wineglasses.

I absolutely couldn't believe it. It was one thing to think that Tom could snow a judge and jury. It would be easy to snow Trey. But how had he snowed me, too? "So you just made it up? You don't think Kay loves him?"

"To tell you the truth," my husband said to me, "I think she does."

At midnight I heard Taffy's soft steps going down the hall to her room. At two o'clock I heard George come in. Both times I woke up only for a second, but after I knew that both of them were back, I slept better. All the chickens home to roost.

Taffy had dinner with Woodrow again on Thursday that week and on Saturday they went to a jazz concert in Durham. "It's good to get out," she said. "It takes my mind off my problems." She still hadn't been able to track down Neddy or Holden, though not from want of trying.

"And that's it?"

"I know the rule of thumb in this house is to fall madly in love by the second course of dinner, but that's not my style. I like Woodrow. We have a good time together. I think for three dates that's pretty good."

"Don't you want to tell me anything about it?"

"Not really," Taffy said, but then she thought about it for a minute. "Okay, I'll tell you this: I get a kick out of the way everybody looks at us, the way the black people and the white people look at us. Not like they're especially scandalized or anything, but they notice, and I think of myself, how if I had seen a couple our age coming into the restaurant, one white and one black, I would have noticed it, too. You see two white people sitting down to dinner, two black people, who cares? But this is different. And I know they're thinking we must have been married for forty years, and that we were probably some big civil-rights trailblazers or something."

"Did you mention it to Woodrow?"

She shook her head. "That's the other thing I like. It doesn't faze him one bit. It's like, whatever bad feelings are out there in the world, he's already seen them and he's over it."

The good news for us was that Woodrow was back working in the basement, and some days he brought enough of a crew to work on the basement and the Florida room. For the first time it seemed possible to me that we would soon be lifted from the yoke of construction.

Kay and Trey seemed to be coming along, too. Nobody mentioned the wedding, I hadn't heard a word from Mrs. Carlson, but they stopped by a couple of times on their way to someplace else. Kay was looking more like her old self, which is to say happy, no mascara, no fabric samples.

In short, the world was coming along nicely. Classes at the studio were full and Taffy was very much in demand. George balanced his time between law school and Erica. Tom was busy at work. Stamp had learned to play dead. I would have been happy to freeze things just the way they were, but when do things ever stay the way you want them to?

The telegram came.

This in itself was an amazing thing to me. I had no idea that there still was such a thing as a telegram. With easy overseas calls and faxes and e-mail, I couldn't even imagine a person wanting to send a telegram, unless, of course, that person didn't want to be reached and didn't want to talk to you.

At any given hour at our house it was possible to be alone and then five minutes later have half a dozen people sitting in the living room. When this particular telegram came (the first and probably last to ever make it to our door), Taffy and I had just come home from school and Tom was already home from work. George was getting ready to go pick up Erica, and Kay and Trey had stopped by on a long hot run they were taking after work. Both of them wore bright blue shorts and orange reflector vests, and with their cheeks flushed from the exercise, they had never looked so completely a pair.

"It's for you," I said to Taffy.

Maybe it was all those war movies, but I couldn't imagine a telegram having anything in it but bad news. My first thought was that Neddy was dead. That the junior executive whose name I could no longer remember was wiring to say he had drowned in a scuba lesson off the coast of Fiji. When Taffy opened the envelope, she fell into a chair before she could have gotten to the end of the page. But the message was short. The whole thing was a very quick read.

JOYFUL TIDINGS STOP JACK AND I
MARRIED TODAY IN CAP FERRET STOP
IMPETUOUS BUT EXACTLY CORRECT
STOP WILL CALL FROM THE HONEY-
MOON STOP WE ARE VERY VERY HAPPY
STOP LOVE HOLDEN.

"Read it out loud," Taffy said. And so I
did.

The room was very quiet. There had been
a lot of emotion these past couple of months,
and now I waited for it to come. I waited for
Kay to break down. Maybe Trey was waiting
for the same thing. We each looked one to
the other, no one wanting to be the one to
say something first.

"Well," George said finally. "There's a big
surprise."

Then Kay smiled and she looped her arm
through Trey's. "Good for them," she said.
"May it last forever."

At that point I started to cry and I think
Trey was getting a little misty, but it was
Taffy who completely broke down.

"What was she thinking of!" Taffy said. "I
have one child and I don't even get to see
her married? What did I do to her that was
so awful?"

Kay went to her aunt and pulled up a
chair beside her and Taffy fell into her

arms and cried great, heartbroken sobs.

It was Holden's wedding, thousands of miles away in the South of France, that tipped the scales. For Kay, it tipped them to certainty: With Jack married off she finally found the conviction in her heart for Trey.

"As soon as you read that telegram, I felt this enormous sense of relief," she said to me the next day over lunch. "It was like I'd been keeping my foot in the door all this time, and as soon as that door was closed, I knew it was the right thing."

"You're not settling?"

"Settling for Trey? How would that even be possible? I look back on that whole thing with Jack and I don't even know what I was thinking of. I meant what I said, I hope they're happy. Maybe two giant egos are like a double negative, they just cancel each other out. I think Holden and Jack were probably made for each other. I think it was my role to find a way for them to meet."

"So the wedding's on?"

"Absolutely, but now I think it's going to be easier. I'm not going to get taken over by Mrs. Carlson. Trey and I will talk it over."

I knew that meant sooner or later we would have to talk about the money, but I'd done such a good job putting it off that I didn't see why I couldn't keep going a little longer.

If Holden's wedding had made Kay realize her own happiness, it threw Taffy into the pit of despair. I could see how much she had pulled herself up since she first came to Raleigh, because now she was back where she had started from. All of her efforts came unraveled. In her mind, her husband was gone and her daughter was gone. In my mind, neither one of them had been there for a long time. Taffy didn't want to teach her classes. She wanted to stay in her room. I came and sat on the edge of her bed.

"What matters is that she's happy," I said.

"Is that all that matters? If that's the case, we might as well say, At least Neddy's happy. This was something I wanted."

"To see her wedding?"

"To plan her wedding. To give her what Mother and Daddy gave me. I know that a wedding should be all about your love for your husband, and I loved Neddy, but the wedding was about me and Mother. The wedding was about how much Mother and I loved each other. I think that's why you could elope. I know you loved Mother, but you weren't ever close to her like I was. We were so close when I was getting married. I would sit next to her on the couch and we'd get a stack of magazines and go through each one page by page. We talked about every dress; we wanted the sleeves off of this one and the train off of that one. We went to

Rich's and picked out my china and silver and crystal. I remember she's the one who found my china pattern. She picked the plate up and she said, Taffy, this is it. I swear, it could have been brown with giant sunflowers on it and I wouldn't have cared. To this day when I think about Mother, those are the times I remember. And I feel like Holden took that from me. It was my one last chance to be a really good mother to her, and she didn't give it to me."

"Oh, baby," I said. "I'm sorry."

"It's different for you and Kay. You're together all the time. You're going to be close to her if she has a thousand people at her wedding or if she gets married at the courthouse on a Wednesday. But Holden's gone. She's been gone since boarding school. All this time I've missed her so much. I just keep thinking, Neddy wouldn't have left me if I'd been a better wife, and Holden wouldn't have married that idiot lawyer if I had been a better mother, and nobody's going to give me the chance to make it right."

I stretched out on the bed next to her and she put her head on my shoulder. "I think you were probably a really great wife and a really great mother. Things just didn't turn out the way you wanted them to."

"On what do you base that opinion?"

I thought about it for a minute. "You're a great sister."

Taffy laughed. "It would certainly be an overstatement to say we always despised each other, but I have no memories of our getting along."

"We're getting along now."

"And in order to do that we had to come all the way around to the beginning. We had to have our bedrooms across the hall from each other again."

"See, every now and then you get a chance to start over."

Unfortunately, Taffy had two chances to start over. After a sufficient amount of moping around the house, she went back to school to teach her classes. It was on one of those afternoons, when I was home alone, that Neddy showed up at the back door.

"Jesus," I said.

"Close," he said, and gave me a mock punch on the arm.

I hadn't seen Neddy in almost two years, but the Neddys of the world change very little. The only difference seemed to be that now he was very tan and the tops of his ears and the bridge of his nose were peeling. He was a big man in every sense of the word — tall, big-boned, and fat all at the same time. His hair had stuck around until about 1980, and by now he was left with only a fringe that he tended to wear too long and a couple of unfortunate scars on his head where they had dug out various basal cell cancers over the years. When he was out of the office, he favored yellow oxford cloth shirts and khaki pants and penny loafers with no socks regardless of the weather. Were it not for the fact that he had dumped my sister, I would have said he was nothing if not consistent.

"Are you coming in?"

The second he set foot inside the door, Stamp came racing around the corner barking like the dog he used to be. Before Neddy had a chance to step back, Stamp had his ankle and was pulling and growling. "There's old Stamp," Neddy said. He reached down, picked the dog up, and turned him counterclockwise until he had no choice but to open his mouth or have his head pop off.

"I'll take him," I said.

Neddy handed him over to me. Stamp was wild, snapping and yapping, minutes away from actually frothing. "That dog never did like me," he said matter-of-factly.

I put Stamp in Taffy's room and shut the door. After a while the barking subsided.

"Are you okay?" I asked Neddy.

He waved his big hand. "Hell, I'm used to it. I buy these pants by the dozen. Some days he'll bite me and some days he won't. You just never know. He hardly ever gets any skin. It's usually just the pants."

Sure enough, his pants were torn. "I

thought he was doing better," I said.

Neddy turned a kitchen chair backward and straddled it. I have almost no memories of seeing Neddy in a chair that was facing the right direction. "I've come to see Taffy," he said.

"I didn't think you were here to see me."

This got a big laugh from him. Neddy liked to make everybody feel like they were the funniest person alive. "You got her stashed in the back?"

"She's working."

This stopped him. "Taffy Bishop has a job other than spending money?"

"She's teaching in my dance studio."

"Teaching what?"

"Well, figure it out. It's a dance studio."

"Taffy can't dance."

"Actually, she can."

He rubbed his big chin with his big hand. "I'll be damned."

"You know she's been wondering what in the hell happened to you. She tracked you as far as Fiji and then you just sort of fell off the map."

"It felt that way."

"Did you hear your daughter got married?"

"Yeah, I talked to her. I wish I'd met the guy. Doesn't seem right, a son-in-law you've never even met."

"He's a prince," I said.

Neddy brightened up. "You know him?"

I told him I did.

"Well, that's good. I'm sure he's fine, then."

It was about that time that Taffy came back. I'm sure if she'd had the chance to write the script, she would have come in wearing black cashmere and a string of pearls, but I thought she looked pretty great in her leotard and jeans. It had been Taffy's intention to lift me up in the world of fashion, but I'm afraid I had pulled her down instead.

"Hello, Ned," was what she said to him. To look at her face, you never would have thought there had been a junior executive or an island called Fiji. You wouldn't have thought she'd tried to call the guy even once. She put down her dance bag and went to the refrigerator.

"Hello, Taffy," Neddy said, his voice stripped of its bravado.

"Posey Martin broke her ankle at the roller rink on Saturday." Taffy stuck her head in the refrigerator and rocked slowly from left to right while she looked around. She came out with an orange. "Her mother stopped in for a refund."

"Poor Posey," I said. Posey was a wispy girl with a bowl haircut. She had been a bad dancer and now it seemed she was a bad skater as well.

"I would think refunds aren't the best

271

policy in a dance studio, but I figured, A broken ankle, cut the kid some slack."

"I would have done it," I admitted.

Taffy leaned up against the counter and sank her fingernails into the rind of the orange. "So," she said to Neddy, "you flew?"

"I wanted to get here as fast as I could."

"You could have walked from Atlanta in the time it took you to get here."

Neddy turned to me. He looked frightened. He was still in the first inning, but things weren't shaping up the way he had expected them to. "Carolina, I don't mean to be rude, but would you mind if Taffy and I went and talked privately?"

I was going to say that was fine. I could stand to go to the bank, anyway. I started to stand up, but Taffy had other ideas.

"If she leaves, then I have to just repeat the whole conversation to her after you go. If she stays, it saves me time. It's like cutting out the middle man."

I sat back down.

"Okay, then," Neddy said. "Okay. Carolina is family, I understand that. Okay. The thing is this, I think you should come home."

It was hardly a declaration of love. It wasn't even an apology. But for Neddy, I'm sure, it had been difficult to come up with.

Taffy peeled back the skin from her orange and then started removing the white pulpy strings. Taffy was very meticulous when it

272

came to oranges. "How was Fiji?"

"Ah, honey, let's not get into that."

It was the kind of thing a husband might say to a wife if she brought up the fact that he had forgotten her birthday five years previously just as he was sitting down to watch the Super Bowl, but given the context here, it seemed a profoundly stupid thing to say.

Taffy's voice got very dark. "I want to know." She popped a section of orange in her mouth.

Neddy rubbed the back of his neck. "Well, I guess we could say if I had loved it, I wouldn't be here."

"You must have loved it a little. You were gone a hell of a long time."

"I had some things I needed to work out over there."

Taffy slammed the orange down on the counter and it blew apart in a thousand bright spots of seed and juice. "Goddammit, Neddy. You're wasting my time."

Neddy was shaken. He wasn't used to being yelled at, especially not by his wife. "What do you want me to tell you? I couldn't get a decent steak to save my life, and the fish was all fried up greasy. A glass of scotch cost twelve bucks, and the fruit didn't look like fruit at all. I ordered a banana for my cereal one morning, and it was about three inches long and three inches around. I didn't like Fiji."

She stared at him. We both stared at him. I had my opinions about Neddy in the past and they weren't so good, but I had no idea how much credit I'd been giving him.

"Go on home," Taffy said finally.

That was when Neddy's mouth started to quiver a little, and it reminded me so much of the way that Kay's big cries started, it frightened me. I couldn't even imagine what a mess there would be if Neddy broke down. "I can't go home without you," he said. "I don't like it there without you. The house doesn't feel right to me anymore. You know you're supposed to be at home. Do you want me to say I was wrong? Okay, I was wrong. I said it. Now cut out all this foolishness."

"What about your girlfriend?"

Now the sunburn was back in Neddy's face and his mouth was really shaking. "I've never known you to be like this," he said. "You never were cruel to me. I told you I was wrong, I told you I didn't like Fiji, and I told you I want you to come home. That's what matters here."

"Did you know that our daughter got married? I've been trying to get ahold of you for weeks."

"Yeah, I know. I talked to her over in France."

"She called you?"

"We didn't talk for very long."

"Do you have her number?"

Neddy reached into his back pocket and pulled out a wallet the size of a Big Mac. I didn't even know how he could sit on it. It looked like he was carrying a couple of thousand dollars in cash, but they could have all been ones. "I've got it in here somewhere." He started to thumb through the bills, laying out various scraps of paper with numbers scrawled on them on the kitchen table. Then suddenly something occurred to him and he scooped them all back up with a sweep of his giant paw. "Come home with me and I'll give you the number."

I knew it was my role to be the silent observer in this affair, but enough was enough. "You want her to forgive you and come home so that she can get a telephone number? That's the pay-off?"

"She wants the number," Neddy said.

"Go home," Taffy said.

Neddy stood up and removed the chair from between his legs. He started to walk toward the door, but then he went over to Taffy and enveloped her in his arms. He swallowed her. She was not a big person and he was huge, and when he folded her up, you couldn't see her at all. "I need you at home, Taffy." He was whispering in her hair. "I make mistakes. You've always known that about me. I always make mistakes. But the General sets me right. You've got to come home and set me right again."

I could hear small, muffled sounds and I knew that Taffy was crying, and I knew that this couldn't be a good thing, but there was nothing I could do about it. I got up and left the room.

chapter fifteen

Tom sliced the pot roast and put it on our plates. It was just the three of us at dinner that night.

"I'm not saying what I'm going to do," Taffy told us. "I'm just saying I'm thinking about it."

I cut into a cooked carrot. I put it in my mouth and chewed. I had no idea what to say.

"Sometimes you get a second chance," Taffy said.

"Sometimes the second chance is with a second person," Tom said.

"Not at my age it isn't."

"You can't be with Neddy just because you're afraid of being alone," I said.

"I don't think that's such an uncommon reason for staying with somebody. Besides, I've learned a lot since I've been here. I think I could do a better job at being married now. I look at the two of you and I think, I could do that."

"With Neddy?"

"I've got thirty-seven years tied up in this thing."

The doorbell rang and Tom got up to answer it. "God, I hope it isn't another telegram," he said.

It was Woodrow. He wasn't wearing a tie tonight, but he looked very nice. Taffy paled at the sight of him.

"Did I get the night wrong?" he said.

"I'm so sorry," she said. "I completely forgot."

Woodrow raised his eyebrows and a slight flash of disappointment crossed his face. "No big deal. It was just a pizza."

"Stay and have some pot roast," Taffy said.

"She made it," Tom said. "It's good. And we already know that you're free for dinner."

So then there were four. It was important to always think of meals as flexible, expandable. I always had something in the freezer that I could throw in just in case the crowd got too big. Tom served up a plate for Woodrow and Taffy got him a glass of wine.

"How's the garage going?" I asked.

"The garage is going well. What's been going on around here today?"

Tom and I stopped to examine our napkins and left any truth or lies that were to be told up to Taffy. "My husband came by," she said.

Woodrow nodded like a man who had just been given a bad diagnosis. "How was he doing?"

Taffy put down her knife and fork and put

her palms flat on the table. "He." She waited for a beat. "Was not so good."

"And he wants you to come back to Atlanta."

"Why do you say that?"

"Because sooner or later even the stupidest man, with all respect to your husband, would wake up and realize what he'd done by letting you go."

It was one of the sweetest things I'd heard anybody say in a long time.

"Thank you," Taffy said quietly.

"So are you going to go?" Woodrow said.

"I'm thinking about it."

"Because you love him?" Woodrow was looking straight at her. He wasn't touching his pot roast. He was going to pin her down, be as specific as Neddy had been vague. He was going to be able to say everything I couldn't say because it wasn't right to try to talk your sister in or out of a marriage. I was glad he had shown up for dinner.

"Because that's my life. That's my home."

"Well, you can have your life there, and if this lawyer is half as good as you say he is, then you can probably have your home, too. What does that have to do with being married?"

"Maybe it has more to do with not being divorced than it does with being married. I don't want to be divorced. I feel like Neddy needs me."

"I'm sure he does, but do you need Neddy? This is your life we're talking about here."

Taffy pushed her hair back and then wrapped her arms around her waist as if she were trying to hold herself in place. "I don't think I want to talk about this anymore."

"That's okay," Woodrow said. "But let me talk for one more minute. I have a vested interest in this thing because I'd like to see you be happy. What you need to ask yourself is this: Are you a better person when you're with him? Are you kinder or smarter or happier? Do you think you do more good in the world? That's what I said to Erica. One man can be perfectly fine, but maybe he doesn't bring out what's good in you, in which case I'd suggest you best not stay with him. But if you find a man who makes you better, or if you're better being on your own, then you need to listen to that."

I looked at Tom, my husband of forty-two years. I knew what Woodrow was talking about. This was a man who had made me better.

Neddy called all the time now. His strategy wasn't to woo her back exactly. He seemed to think he'd get her back by showing her what a desperate mess he was without her. He called because the electricity had been cut off, and then he called from his cell phone because the phone went dead as well. He claimed not to understand why. He called about trash pickup, a sore tooth, and once, in the very depths of neediness, a broken shoelace. Should he just throw the shoes out? he wanted to know.

"He's making this up," I said.

"Don't be so sure," Taffy said.

Even though she took the calls and dispensed her advice, I think it was Woodrow's words that were making their way inside her head more than Neddy's. She had dinner with Woodrow almost every night now. She came in later and later. Then one fine afternoon Woodrow emerged from the basement and said our foundation was secure.

"We'll have the Florida room finished in two weeks, absolute maximum."

"Electrical sockets and everything?" I asked.

"Everything."

I could hardly believe it. Woodrow had never promised a finishing date before. We were moving out of construction. I wondered if he would still come by in the morning for coffee on his way to other jobs. It was one more reason to hope that Taffy didn't go back to Neddy.

Taffy didn't talk about Neddy, no matter how much she may have thought about him. She wasn't the kind of person to engage in long bouts of "What if?" and "What do you think?" If she was worried about what to do with her life, she kept it to herself. She wound up doing what I had done all my life when I didn't know what to do: She poured herself into dancing. Taffy worked harder and harder at school. She bought a television set and a VCR for the studio and would watch tap-instruction videos after the students had left so she could teach herself new steps that she could pass on to them. She would watch Fred Astaire and Eleanor Powell and Gene Kelly movies and rewind the dance scenes over and over again while she tapped along. She said she wanted to be reincarnated as Ann Miller, but I thought she resembled no one as much as the young Buddy Ebsen; everything about her was so incredibly easy and loose, as if at any minute she might sail up the wall, her feet as light and fast as wings.

Taffy received a couple of postcards from Holden and Jack, one sent from Cap Ferret and another from a small town on the Italian coast. Holden said they had rented a boat, that they were eating persimmons, and that they would be coming home soon. Work, she said, had gotten completely out of control in her absence.

"What are you going to say to her when she comes back?" I asked.

"By the time she comes back," Taffy said, "I think I'll be over it."

Sometimes, when Taffy needed a partner, she would ask George to come to the studio and dance with her. He was happy to do it. He missed teaching his class even though he didn't have the time for it now. They would tap together in wide circles across the empty studio, their feet rattling out such perfect staccato time that when the tape was over, they didn't stop to put another one on. George was a relentless dancer and he took a certain pleasure in trying to run Taffy into the ground. She could go pretty far, and then finally she'd throw up her hands and scream, collapsing into a heap on the floor. "You're too good," she said. "And you're too damn young."

"Get up," he said, his feet still slapping and riffing.

"I'm dead. You've killed me."

So then George and I would go a couple of rounds. I was sorry he was going to be a lawyer. I couldn't help myself. I didn't understand how anyone could dance as well as George and not want to make it his life's work. When we were all three lying on the hardwood floor in puddles of our own sweat, George rolled over on his stomach and looked at us.

"I've got to tell you something," he said.

"What?"

"I'm going to ask Erica to marry me."

Taffy and I both sat up, light-headed from

exhaustion but suddenly, fully alert. "*Another wedding?*" Taffy said.

George shook his head. "Just an engagement, I swear. We wouldn't get married for at least two years. We both want to finish school first and we don't have the money to live together."

"So why not wait?" I asked. "I mean, I'm happy for you, don't get me wrong, but is there a hurry?" I hoped I was happy for him. I wanted to be happy for him, but George and Erica were so impossibly young, despite my own personal history. If they really did wait two years, that would be better. Twenty-seven sounded more marriageable than twenty-five.

"I just want her to know, I want everyone to know, this is absolutely it for me. This is the woman I'm going to marry even if we can't do it right now. I just wanted to tell you first, what with everything that happened with Holden and Jack, and I don't think this is the time for any more surprises in the family. I was going to wait and tell you and Dad tonight, but I don't know, dancing always makes me think about getting married now. Everything makes me think about getting married."

"How could it not?" Taffy said. "It's all anybody in this family ever talks about." She put her sweaty hands together and pulled one of them over the other. "Here," she said, and slid something bright and shiny across the floor in George's direction. "Give her this."

George held it up to the light. It was Taffy's engagement ring.

"I'd have it reset," she said. "Just to make it Erica's, but there's no bad luck in the diamond. Diamonds are too hard to absorb bad luck. It's part of their charm."

"I can't take this," George said.

"Of course you can."

"What would Neddy say?"

Taffy smiled and looked at her hand. There was just a little platinum band there now. It looked nice, simpler. "Neddy would never notice it was missing. Anyway, Neddy and I are getting a divorce, so I won't be wearing it."

"You're getting a divorce?" I said.

"I called Buddy Lewis yesterday."

"Were you going to tell me?"

"I wanted to try it on by myself first, see how it felt." She shrugged. "It feels okay."

I scooted over next to George and looked at the beginnings of Taffy's married life. "I remember the day you got that ring," I said. "Mother called me over to the house so I could come see it. You were so excited you could barely hold your hand still. I thought it was the most gorgeous, frivolous thing I'd ever seen in my life."

"You don't remember the day I got that ring," she said. "It was seven years ago, it was at Tiffany's, and I picked it out myself. That is actually my fourth engagement ring. Neddy let me get a new one every ten years. He called it my upgrade."

"But shouldn't you give this to Holden?" George said. He was turning the ring from side to side. Now that he was holding it, he wanted it.

"She can have the other ones."

"You kept the other ones?" George said.

"Of course I did. A diamond doesn't mean anything, not in the long run. That's why your mother never bothered with them, which is why she doesn't have one to give to you now."

"You're wrong," George said. "It means a lot."

"It means a lot to you, right now. That's why I want you to have it."

The next week we had four reasons to have a party: Kay and Trey set the date for their wedding, George and Erica announced their engagement, Holden and Jack came back from France married, and the Florida room was finished if not paid for. We would need to invite all of the Woodrow girls, and their families, and Jack's family, and Trey's family, and all of their friends. By the time the guest list reached one hundred and fifty, we decided instead to simply reassemble the crowd from Taffy's birthday party and have a little dinner party at which to discuss larger parties that would follow in the future. Still, Erica thought we should have invitations, and so she wrote each one by hand.

~~~

Caroline McSwain and Tom McSwain and
Taffy Bishop and Felix Woodrow
Invite you to a celebration of the marriage of
Holden and Jack Carroll
and the engagements of
Katherine McSwain and Trey Bennett
and
Erica Woodrow and George McSwain

~

Saturday evening at 7 p.m.
Casual

~~~

She had elegant, sloping handwriting. The diamond ring sparkled on her hand as it moved across the paper. When she finished with one invitation, she would lay it out on the dining-room table and start the next.

"But that's all of us," Taffy whispered to me. "There's no one coming who isn't on the invitation."

"I like doing them," Erica said, keeping her eyes on the work at hand.

Holden and Jack waltzed in as if they had only just been to the corner to pick up a carton of milk. They were both casual and golden. Jack had shaved and was wearing a new suit. Holden wore a short suede skirt and kept her legs bare. Holden and Taffy fell into each other's arms as if nothing had happened at all. "Mother, I only wish you could have been there," Holden said. "We were on the beach at sunset, barefoot. It was the most beautiful wedding."

"I wish I could have been there, too," Taffy said.

We took everyone in to see the Florida room. We didn't have the furniture in there yet, but it was finished, beautiful, and perfectly clean.

"Daddy's a genius," Erica said. Taffy took Woodrow's arm.

"And speaking of genius, you," Holden said to Kay. "Now you really are my favorite cousin."

"I was just glad to help," Kay said. She kissed Jack on the cheek as if he were a distant, little-remembered relative, which, I suppose, he was.

"When are you getting married?" Jack asked George.

I don't think George had quite forgiven Jack. He put his arm around Erica and

288

pulled her close to him. "We're going to wait at least two years. It's so great to be engaged, there isn't any point in rushing it."

Jack smiled and tapped George on the chest. "You think it's great being engaged, you should try getting married."

"With the new engagement averaging law between family members, it will mean that we were both engaged a year," Holden said to George.

"When are you getting married?" Jack asked Kay. "It seems like you've been engaged forever."

"That's because you've been so busy lately," Kay said. "Remember Einstein's Theory of Relativity? Time moves at different rates of speed depending on what you're doing."

"A little less than a year."

"Eight months from now," Trey said, answering the question. He turned to Erica. "Maybe we should have a double wedding. I understand that's the kind of thing they do in musicals."

"Are we living a musical now?"

Woodrow put his hands on his daughter's shoulders. "With all due respect to your generous offer, I don't think we could afford to take on half of your wedding."

"No, really, the whole thing's paid for. The more the merrier."

Tom and I both heard the sentence and we

stepped in the direction of that particularly interesting conversation.

"Your wedding is already paid for?" Taffy said. God bless Taffy, she'd jump right in there.

"Well, we're paying for it. I certainly would be happy to have Erica and George share it with us."

"You're paying for it?" Tom said, trying to keep the incredulity out of his voice.

"Okay, let's be honest here," Kay said. "Trey's paying for it. I'll buy the Jordan almonds or something. Daddy, why are you looking at me like that?"

"Mrs. Bennett told your parents that they would be paying for half the wedding," Taffy said. I was grateful. I don't think I would have been able to explain it quite so succinctly.

"That's insane!" Kay laughed and took a sip of champagne. "You would have been completely wiped off the map even paying half. Do you have any idea what this thing is going to cost?"

"Some idea," Tom said weakly.

"This is awful," Trey said. "I guess my mother and I have never talked about it. I always planned to pay for the wedding. She doesn't talk to me about wedding details. She never should have talked to you about money, though."

"And you never even told me?" Kay put

her arm around my shoulder. "Why didn't you talk to me about this? You must have been going out of your mind."

"It seems funny now," I said. "Or it will seem funny soon."

"Maybe you should think about this generous offer," Woodrow said to Erica.

"Every girl wants her own wedding," Erica said. "Unless she's in a musical."

"Where do we even start the toasts?" Tom said, raising his glass.

"To my daughter and her husband on a day several days after their wedding day," Taffy said. "I wish you every happiness in the world."

"To my daughter and her husband-to-be on their engagement," Woodrow said. "I could not be more proud or more pleased."

"To our daughter and her husband-to-be," I said. "May tonight be the beginning of the happiest time of your life."

grand finale

On the morning of the biggest wedding that Raleigh had ever seen, I got out of bed at six o'clock. I had been awake since two, the endless list of Mrs. Carlson's instructions playing over in my head to the tune of "My Favorite Things." Tom, bless his soul, was sound asleep. I had been watching him for hours in the little bit of light thrown out by our electric clock, thinking of how glad I was to be married to him and how smart we had been for starting our life together the way we did. I don't think I could have stood up to all that Kay would have to face today, everyone she had ever known and everyone she didn't know coming to see her looking beautiful. But Kay was a different sort of person than I was. For all her sentimentality, she had proven herself to be someone who knew how to stand up under pressure. She would be wonderful. The day would be wonderful. Too many ironclad plans had been laid down for me to have any doubts about that.

In a hotel across town my two oldest boys, Henry and Charlie, were sleeping with their wives, while their children slept around them in foldaway cots. Every cousin and uncle and aunt, every college roommate and childhood confidant was assembled. The wedding wasn't until six o'clock but, of course, there was a brunch at noon and then meticulously organized trips to the hairdresser. Whatever time I was going to have to myself I was going to have right now, and so quietly, quietly, I sneaked out of the room and went to the kitchen.

Taffy was there.

"God, you scared me to death," I said.

"I still have a key," she said. Taffy had bought a condominium six months ago and had moved her furniture up from Atlanta.

"What are you doing here so early?"

"I knew you'd be up. I've only been here for half an hour."

"I've been up since two," I said.

She handed me a cup of coffee. "Drink this and go get dressed. There's something I want us to do."

"This morning? At six a.m.?"

"Go get dressed," she said.

Taffy was wearing a leotard and a loose skirt, so I went and put on the same thing. When I came out again, we left the house like a couple of thieves who had changed their minds about taking anything and we snuck off to her car.

"Are we going to the studio?"

"Just try to go along with this, okay?"

"Okay, but I'm not up for a surprise party."

"Neither am I."

"Did you have a good time at the rehearsal dinner?"

"It certainly was, what's the word? Enormous?"

"Your date looked nice."

"You can take Woodrow anywhere. He's looking forward to the wedding," Taffy said. She looked at me out of the corner of her eye. "Are you nervous?"

"Am I supposed to be nervous?"

"It's a big day." The streets around our house were empty and just turning pink in the early May light. Everywhere I looked there were flowers and tender leaves. The whole city was dressed for a wedding.

"I'd be nervous if I thought Kay wasn't doing the right thing, but she is. The rest of it, the party, that will all be fine."

"I thought I was going to envy you, your daughter having the huge wedding. But now that it's here, I'm glad it's you and not me." Taffy pulled the car up in front of McSwan's. It had been a long time since I'd been there so early in the morning. Somehow the place looked smaller without all the cars. We got out of the car and Taffy unlocked the door and flipped on the lights. I looked at the pale, scuffed floors. I looked at our reflection in the mirror. It was too early for such big mirrors.

"So," I said. "Are you going to give me a pep talk?"

"Nope." She went over and put a tape in the player. A big-band version of "Putting on the Ritz" came through the speakers. "We're going to dance."

She sat down on the floor and took out two pairs of shoes. With a little red screwdriver that said *McSwan's* on the side, she tightened up our taps, tight but not too tight, so they'd have just the right amount of resonance. I had given her the screwdriver as a present when she bought me out of half the dance school. She had needed to invest part of the avalanche of money that came with getting divorced. She slid me my shoes.

I started to tell her that this wasn't the time to dance, that there was too much to do, but as soon as I heard the music, I knew she was exactly right.

"If you're blue and you don't know where to go to, why don't you go where fashion sits?" — *beat, beat* — "Putting on the Ritz!" Taffy sang. She was up and dancing before I had my shoes all the way buckled, and then a minute later I was with her. She led the routine and I followed, at first one step behind and then catching up. Syncopated pull-backs, wings, and shuffles, Maxi Fords and step ball change, and running flaps so fast it made us laugh. We cut wide circles around the room, our arms sailing out to the side. There was nothing in the world like hearing the music your own feet made, nothing like feeling that your body was the instrument. I had been dancing since I was six years old, and whenever I was dancing, really dancing, I felt as good as I had felt about it when I was a child. There would be dancing at the end of this day, a big band and a thousand people crowded on a floor. But it wasn't anything like this. Now I was flying, now I was completely, happily lost inside my own feet.

We danced for nearly an hour. Taffy had brought every song I loved. When finally it was time to go, we took off our shoes and stretched out on the barre.

"We could have been Fred and Adele Astaire," she said.

"We could have been the Nicholas Brothers," I said.

"We should have been doing this all along," Taffy said, her hair slicked back with sweat. "We would have made a great team."

It was true. It would have been great if Taffy and I had been dancing together from the beginning. "But isn't it something that we're doing it now?" I said.

acknowledgments

Thanks to my family: They are ever-patient, loving, and supportive. I learn from them daily.

Thanks to my friends: They offer me their endless grace.

Thanks to Shaye Areheart and Lisa Bankoff: They have become both family and friends, and they do it all.

about the author

Jeanne Ray works as a registered nurse at the Frist Clinic in Nashville, Tennessee. She is married and has two daughters. Together, she and her husband have ten grandchildren. She is the best-selling author of *Julie and Romeo*.